BIG, BAD MISTER WOLFE

H. L. Macfarlane

This one's for me.

PROLOGUE

Scarlett

There were wolves in the woods. Everyone knew it. You could hear them, howling mournfully in the distance, and then you'd know to keep away from the trees. When they were quiet the people of Rowan could venture through, though they rarely dared to go alone.

But the townsfolk were fearful of travelling too deeply into the woods regardless of whether they could hear the howls or not. The mere thought that just one hungry, smiling, loping wolf might be out to get them was enough to stop most folk from straying off the beaten path that wound through the trees.

But not Scarlett Duke.

For Scarlett's grandmother lived deep in the woods, at least an hour from the outskirts of Rowan. Nobody knew why the kindly old lady chose to live so far from the town and her wealthy son's family. There were rumours that she had fought with her daughter-in-law and that she was kicked out of the house as a result.

But that was only a rumour.

Scarlett loved visiting her grandmother and was often sent to her little house in the woods laden with supplies for the woman. Her mother, Frances, never let her take her younger twin brothers with her, though they longed to explore with their older sister, who doted upon them. Her mother said it was because it was too dangerous, though Scarlett had been travelling through the woods since she was younger than her brothers were now.

Sometimes Scarlett wondered why her mother treated her differently than her two brothers. Where she was warm and generous with Rudy and Elias, she was cold and distant with Scarlett. But she was never cruel, and Scarlett wanted for nothing, so she loved her mother deeply anyway.

Her father, on the other hand, lavished attention on his only daughter, though not in front of his wife. He spoiled Scarlett, sneaking her extra dessert after dinner, taking her out riding on weekends and buying her new dresses when she didn't need them.

Richard Duke was the wealthiest man in town and respected by many. But by virtue of being the wealthiest man in town, and having a daughter who was fast approaching womanhood, many men had begun approaching Scarlett's father vying to marry her to their sons, in the hopes of joining their families together. Scarlett didn't like this...not least because her mother's face twisted into a scowl whenever someone brought it up.

Scarlett sighed heavily in front of the mirror that adorned her dressing table. She didn't look much like her mother, instead inheriting the pale skin, dark hair and blue eyes of her father, whilst Rudy and Elias both had burnished copper curls and green eyes. Frances Duke didn't seem to appreciate that only Scarlett looked like her father, though it wasn't as if her daughter could do anything about this.

And now she was sixteen. Scarlett could see the last vestiges of her childhood disappearing from her face. Her cheeks had lost their baby fat. The Cupid's bow of her lips had become more pronounced. Her lashes had grown in thick and long and fluttering. Her chest and hips were filling out whilst her waist stayed small, and her dark, wavy hair grew long and shiny. She knew, objectively, that she was a pretty girl, but all she yearned for was the tall, willowy frame, golden hair and green eyes of her mother.

Thinking that some fresh air would help her feel better, Scarlett laced up a deep red dress over her white petticoat, sliding on a pair of delicate slippers before casting one final glance at her own reflection. She opened her door as quietly as possible and crept past her brothers' bedroom, since they were both long-since asleep. But just as she reached the bottom of the stairs and made to enter the kitchen to inform her parents that she was going to step outside for a while, the sound of her mother's voice gave her pause.

"Richard, you promised! You swore and you swore that you would send her away, and now you say you won't?"

"My love, Scarlett's done nothing wrong! Why must you punish her for my mistake?"

"She doesn't need to have done anything wrong," her mother scoffed. "Have you seen the men lining up for her hand? I won't have our sons' inheritance put at risk because that whore you slept with gifted you with a beautiful daughter!"

Scarlett froze. What on earth were they talking about?

Her father sounded pained as he said, "Frances, she wasn't a whore. You know that. She –"

"But she wasn't me, was she? I wasn't enough for you back then, and you took it out on me by taking that woman's daughter in."

11

"It wasn't like that, Frances. Our parents knew I never wanted an arranged marriage. I was acting out. But I love you. I came to love you and that's all that should matter."

"If you loved me you wouldn't have taken Scarlett in."

Scarlett didn't know what to think. Her mother's aloof attitude towards her made far more sense to her now, though.

That didn't make her feel any better.

"What was I supposed to do? Her mother disappeared. She had no-one else."

"So you give her to another family! You don't shame me by bringing her here."

Her father sighed heavily. "She's my daughter, Frances. I love her, and she's dear to Rudy and Elias. I cannot throw her out."

"I'm not asking you to! I'm asking you to send her to her grandmother's. I want her out of sight, and not in line to inherit what are rightfully your sons' fortunes. Lord knows the woman will be happy to have her; she's always been her favourite."

"If you'd let my mother see Rudy and Elias more often –"

"What, in that wolf-infested forest? I think not."

"Frances –"

"Please, Richard," she pleaded. "Just send Scarlett away. I can't bear watching her grow up to look more like you than our sons ever will. Just send her away."

There was a long, conflicted pause, during which Scarlett hardly dared to breathe.

"...as you wish," her father said eventually, his voice sad and resigned. "But let me have one more day with her. I shall send her away after that."

Scarlett didn't hear the rest of the conversation. She fled the corridor, opening the door with trembling hands as she flung herself into the cold, spring evening.

She didn't know where she was going at first, her manic feet scrabbling across the dark, empty road through Rowan. Scarlett's brain was numb; she didn't have the capacity to process what had just occurred. What she had heard. What she had learned.

Her entire life had been a lie.

Before she knew it Scarlett had reached the woods, her breath coming out in little puffs as she shivered slightly. It was only early April, after all, and the night air stung her face. But Scarlett couldn't turn back now. She couldn't face her father – let alone the woman who had always been her mother – when she felt like this.

No. She'd go precisely where they had intended to send her, anyway.

To her grandmother's.

Sincerely wishing she had thought to wrap herself up in one of her expensive cloaks before leaving, Scarlett steeled herself for the hour-long walk along the winding road that eventually led to her grandmother's lonely house.

But Scarlett had never walked through the woods at night before. The place she loved so much felt unfamiliar and eerie, as if one of the long, slender shadows created by the trees might reach out and grab her.

And then she heard it.

The howling.

The wolves, Scarlett thought in sudden, abject terror. She had forgotten the one and only rule even her 'mother' had insisted upon her following – do not enter the woods when the wolves are heard. For the first time in her short life, Scarlett thought that she might die. That this would be her end, pitiful and tragic though it was.

But Scarlett didn't want this to be her end. Hitching up the skirt of her dress, and ignoring the blisters beginning to form on her feet from wearing such insubstantial shoes for a hike through the woods, Scarlett picked up her pace and began to jog along the road.

The howls only grew more and more frequent as she headed deeper into the forest. And they were louder, too, echoing all around until the only sound Scarlett could hear were the soulful, eerie cries of the wolves pacing in the darkness. When she was just ten minutes away from her grandmother's house she was sure she could pick out the tell-tale yellow eyes of the creatures, stalking her every footstep through the woods. Their woods.

"I don't want to die," she cried out silently, the words barely creating a cloud of chilly air in front of Scarlett's face.

When she ran straight into someone her scream was not-so-silent, but a hand was quick to cover her mouth and quell the noise just as she felt another on her back, keeping her from falling.

"You have a funny way of showing you don't want to die, little miss," a man growled softly. "What are you doing out here?"

Scarlett hardly dared to look at the man currently holding her up. But she had to; she knew she did. It was too dark to see him properly, though even if it had been bright as day Scarlett would only have taken notice of his eyes.

Amber, like the wolves.

Scarlett fought against him, desperate to pull away for some innate, visceral reason. But the man only held her tighter; then, when the wolves howled once more, pulled her against his chest. Scarlett's heart was hammering so painfully the stranger was bound to feel it. She was too frightened to care.

"Best get you to your grandmother's, Miss Scarlett," he murmured, his voice low and melodic as his strange eyes bored into her own, "else you're liable to get eaten."

Blindly Scarlett allowed the man who somehow knew her to pull her along by the hand, ripping through the trees instead of taking the road without sparing another glance Scarlett's way.

She dared not let go. She knew that if she did it would be the end of her.

When finally she spied the silhouette of her grandmother's house Scarlett could barely breathe, her vision as red as her dress whilst her lungs felt like they were being torn apart. As soon as the pair of them reached the front door the howling of the wolves abated, many of them whining in disappointment. They would not risk getting so close to Scarlett's grandmother's house. They never had.

In the warm light of the lantern hanging above the door Scarlett could finally look at her saviour. He wore a dark cloak over equally dark clothes which matched the ebony of his hair, though a solitary streak of white had broken through the black. But despite that the man could not have been much older than his mid-twenties, going by his relatively unlined face. A small scar split his left eyebrow in two.

And those eyes. In the light those deep amber eyes looked no less unnatural. And they were staring at Scarlett as intently as she was staring at the man they

16

belonged to.

It was only then that Scarlett realised she recognised him as a travelling merchant from the market and clearly why, in turn, he had known who she was. But then the door of her grandmother's house was thrown open, and the woman herself stared at the pair of them with surprise written all over her face.

"Adrian Wolfe, what are you doing on my doorstep with – Red, my goodness! My love, what are you doing here so late?"

Scarlett still hadn't caught her breath. She found her eyes flailing wildly from Adrian's face to her grandmother's as she struggled to vocalise her thoughts.

"I found her close by," Adrian explained, sounding as if he hadn't just run full-pelt through the forest with a young woman in tow. "Someone ought to tell her it's dangerous out here."

"And they have. Get in here, Red! You're freezing – what were you doing out here in clothes like that? You're barely dressed! And Mr Wolfe –"

But the man had disappeared in the time it had taken her to usher Scarlett inside.

"Typical merchant, travelling here and there without so much as a warning," her grandmother tutted. "I should ask him what he was doing out here, this close to my house. We're so far from Rowan! You'd think he'd have learned his lesson about how dangerous the woods

17

are by now."

But Scarlett could barely take in anything her grandmother was saying, numb and shocked as she was. A wave of exhaustion quite suddenly washed over her and so, without saying a word, Scarlett retired to bed and fell into a troubled, dark and fitful sleep.

That night she dreamed of wolves, amber eyes, and a woman who left a baby and ran away.

CHAPTER ONE

Scarlett

Scarlett reached her eighteenth birthday faster than she could have ever thought possible. Two years spent living in the woods with her grandmother after her brush with the wolves had been easy and peaceful and happy... so long as she didn't think about the rest of her family.

For although Scarlett had seen and even conversed with her father and 'mother' since she had run away in the dead of night, and had played with her little brothers on the occasions they were brought along to market at the same time as her, Scarlett was very much separated from the rest of the Dukes. It was a miserable feeling, especially when her father failed to elaborate any further on the nature of Scarlett's existence. She knew he was doing this to spare his wife's feelings, and though often Scarlett resented the way the woman was acting she could hardly blame her.

I'm a threat to her sons and to her marriage, Scarlett reminded herself on a regular basis. *Frances is not wrong to want me out of the picture.*

And it was hardly as if she had been kicked out onto the streets. Heidi Duke – Scarlett's grandmother – was a warm and generous person. And though her house was small and isolated it was by no means impoverished. It was...ordinary. Grounded. Safe.

Which was exactly what Scarlett needed to forget about the circumstances of her birth.

"Are you planning to sleep all morning, Red?" her grandmother called out, startling Scarlett. She had always called her Red, ever since Scarlett was a little girl. She loved the nickname, though thinking about how Rudy and Elias also called her by the moniker made her sad, since she rarely heard their voices now.

"One moment, Nana!" Scarlett replied, hurrying with the laces on her boots before bolting through to the kitchen. When her grandmother saw her generally dishevelled appearance she smiled kindly whilst rolling her eyes.

"You can't go into town looking like that, my love. Have you even combed your hair?"

Scarlett shrugged. Most of the time she kept her hair tied back and out of the way. It served no purpose for her to have it down. And besides, she wanted to draw as little attention to herself as possible, and if that meant keeping up a plain appearance then so be it.

"Come now, Scarlett, you're eighteen now. *Eighteen!* You can't be looking like this now you're a woman."

"What does it matter, Nana?" she replied as she was motioned to sit in a chair. Her grandmother got out a comb and began to run it through Scarlett's long, wavy hair. "If any man were to find out they don't *actually* get a portion of the Duke fortune then they'd turn tail and run away from me as fast as wolves!"

"I somehow doubt that, dear," her grandmother murmured. And then, in exasperation, "Do you take no pride in yourself at all? You still have all those beautiful dresses your father sent over for you."

Scarlett winced as her grandmother worked out a knot in her hair.

"They're not practical for working in, are they?"

"Ah, because I get you to help with such strenuous manual labour, of course."

From the window the two of them heard a snort of laughter.

21

Her grandmother raised an eyebrow. "Is that you, Samuel?"

The man popped his head up, cheeks red with embarrassment. "Yes, ma'am. My apologies; I didn't mean to sneak about. Ah – morning, Miss Scarlett. Happy birthday!"

"Morning, Sam."

Samuel Birch's family ran a mill; Scarlett's grandmother had hired him to do all of her heavy lifting, such as wood cutting, gardening, repairing the roof and helping Scarlett carry supplies back from the market. Scarlett was fond of the young man, whose sandy hair, green eyes and tanned skin reminded her of her little brothers.

There was nothing *little* about Sam, though. He had grown big and well-built like his father; Scarlett had once witnessed him carry three sacks of flour over his shoulders like they were nothing.

"Right, my love, head back through to your bedroom and put on that red dress you used to love so much. Yes, the one with the white petticoat. And put some colour on your lips! I have a present for you when you're ready."

Scarlett knew there was no arguing with her grandmother on the subject so she gave Sam one, final smile before retreating back through to her room to change. But she didn't want to unlace her boots, nor remove the thick, woollen tights she was wearing. Rowan had been hit by a bout of cold, nasty weather that was only just beginning to dissipate. Though it was a gloriously sunny, early April day today, snow still lay on the ground and the air bit at Scarlett's cheeks.

Thinking that her grandmother would simply have to accept a compromise, Scarlett shirked out of everything but her tights and boots and carefully redressed in the petticoat and red dress she had originally worn two years ago when she'd been saved by Adrian Wolfe.

Scarlett hadn't thought about the man for a while. Or, at least, she had tried not to. The merchant was only in Rowan once a month so Scarlett found it fairly easy to avoid him. She didn't know *why* she was avoiding him – she still hadn't even thanked him for saving her life, which Scarlett knew was desperately rude.

But there was something about Adrian Wolfe that scared her. Perhaps it was his eyes. Or maybe it was the fact that he'd been prowling through the woods at night, just like the wolves had been doing, and had caught her.

But if he hadn't I'd be dead, Scarlett thought as she finished lacing up her dress and moved to her dressing table. She picked up a pot of red pigment and a tiny brush – a previous gift from her grandmother – and proceeded to carefully paint her lips. Though her grandmother continually insisted upon it Scarlett rarely wore the stuff; there was an association between painted lips and witchcraft amongst the townspeople that she'd rather avoid.

The thought used to scare her, and painting her lips certainly didn't help Scarlett to blend into the crowd, but for some reason now she was beginning to feel bold. Her grandmother had told her to take greater care of her appearance because she was of marrying age. Scarlett didn't care for that but, perhaps now that she was an adult, she could be free to be whomever she pleased for *herself*. And maybe who she wanted to be was a woman who dressed in the colour of her name and wore her hair down her back and smiled mysteriously at strangers.

But Scarlett couldn't help but laugh at the notion, watching as her red-lipped reflection did the same. She certainly looked the part for the fantasy. She merely lacked the confidence and backbone to do it. And, at the end of the day, she didn't care for being a beautiful, mysterious woman. All she wanted was to be accepted back into her family.

"I guess one day as someone different needn't hurt," she mumbled as she ran her fingers through her long, soft hair. With her dark lashes, pale skin and red lips, Scarlett had to admit that she liked her reflection, even though it still pained her to look nothing like her brothers and Frances Duke.

With a swish of her skirts she headed back through to the kitchen where Sam, who was currently leaning on the windowsill drinking a cup of tea prepared for him by her grandmother, gawked at the sight of her.

"Miss – Miss Scarlett, you look –"

"Beautiful," her grandmother beamed, though she frowned when she saw Scarlett's boots.

"There's still snow on the ground, Nana," Scarlett reasoned. "Boots make sense."

"I suppose I can let you off with that *today.* But from now on I want to see you put this much effort into your appearance every day, Red. You have a family name to uphold, whether that wife of my useless son wants to acknowledge you or not."

Scarlett smiled softly as she watched the lined, aged face of her grandmother grow harsh with contempt. When Scarlett had finally explained to her why she had run off at night two years ago, her grandmother had wanted to march over to the Duke household the very next day to shout at her son. But Scarlett had begged her not to – not for her sake but for her brothers.

"If it will make you happy then I'll try to look a little better, Nana," Scarlett said.

The woman's dark expression finally disappeared, and she smiled. "Come over here, Red," she murmured, gesturing for Scarlett to follow her over to the chest she kept by the front door. Inside was lying a large pile of thick, deep crimson fabric.

Scarlett stared at her grandmother. "What is this?"

"Pick it up and see."

With delicate hands Scarlett picked up the fabric,

discovering that it was a cloak complete with a white, fur-lined hood.

"I've never seen this before."

"That's because I haven't worn it since before I was married. Seems a shame to let it go to waste when I have such a beautiful grand-daughter who could use it."

"Nana, I can't!" Scarlett protested. "This is yours. I can't take it from you."

But her grandmother merely waved away her comments. "Nonsense! And you've needed a new cloak for a while, now. May as well have one of your own instead of relying on that useless father of yours, right? Come on, my love, try it on!"

She was wrapping Scarlett up in the fabric and tying it across her breastbone before Scarlett could protest further. The material was heavy; the fur that tickled her neck surprisingly soft.

"What's the fur from, Nana?" she asked curiously, twirling slightly to appreciate the way the cloak spun around her feet.

"It's the undercoat of a wolf. Softest fur you'll ever get around these parts."

"Oh." Something about literally wearing a wolf somewhat unsettled Scarlett but she pushed the feeling to the side for now. She smiled for her grandmother and curtsied slightly for Sam, who had watched her put on the cloak in numb silence, his tea long since forgotten. "How do I look?"

"Like a Duke," her grandmother said proudly. "Like a beautiful, confident woman. What do you think, Samuel?"

"Huh? Oh, I – Miss Scarlett, you look wonderful!"

Scarlett couldn't help but giggle at Sam's bumbling compliment. She had known him for two years and in that time she had never seen him struggle with his words *quite* as much as he currently was. There was something deeply satisfying about it.

She reached up to unhook a basket from the wall. "I best be off to market before Mr Beck is out of bread."

"Ah, Miss Scarlett, would you like a hand?"

Scarlett shook her head. "That's okay, Sam. And I'm sure my grandmother needs you here." She kissed the woman on her cheek as she opened the front door and felt the cold spring air hit her face. It was refreshing, and brought a flash of colour to Scarlett's face.

"Be sure to pick up some cake from Charles, too!" her grandmother called out after her. "It *is* your birthday, after all!"

Scarlett waved a hand in acknowledgement as she made her way down the winding, twisting road through the woods. On a beautiful, golden morning such as today, with the sun turning the frost dusting the trees to diamonds and birds filling the air with song, Scarlett could hardly believe how terrified she'd been of the very same place when she'd turned sixteen.

Unbidden she thought once more of Adrian Wolfe and his strange, strange eyes. They belonged in a dream, just like the night itself. He wasn't a man that Scarlett wanted to think about when the sun was out and she was dressed in red, informing the world that she was alive and she was there and she was grown.

And yet, even still, as Scarlett made her way into the town of Rowan, she couldn't help but secretly hope that the man would be there.

Secretly.

CHAPTER TWO

Adrian

"She's really grown up nicely, ain't she, Gerold?"

"And eighteen now, too! She'll be swarming in marriage requests soon, no doubt."

"But didn't she get sent to live with her grandmother instead of living in the main house? Why was that?"

"It don't matter – she's still his daughter!"

Adrian Wolfe had tried to avoid the inane chatter of the two merchants who'd travelled into town with him.

Honestly, he had. But the men had been talking about the same person for over ten minutes now as they finished setting up their stalls, and even Adrian could admit he was curious.

"Who're you talking about?" he asked politely, keeping his face as blandly curious as possible.

Gerold Rogers stared at him in disbelief. "Why, Scarlett Duke, of course! I know you're only through here once a month but you can't have missed her, Wolfe!"

Of course Adrian knew Scarlett Duke. She had run into his arms in the dark of night, in the middle of the woods, just two years earlier. It had seemed like something out of a fairytale or a dream – a young, beautiful and terrified woman lost and alone at the mercy of wolves.

And more than one kind, at that, Adrian thought in amusement, though he kept his expression blank as he nodded at Gerold in acknowledgement.

"Ah, you're right. I know her. Does all the errands for Heidi."

"Didn't know you were on first name terms with the old lady, Wolfe," the other man, Frank Holt, replied.

"I've done business with her on more than a few occasions. She has a pretty great stock of rare herbs from the mountains that I like, though lord knows how she got them in the first place."

"She's a good girl through and through," Gerold continued on wistfully, talking about Scarlett once more. "I wish all the young folk looked after their elders like she does Old Lady Duke. I'd be content if I had a lovely girl like her looking after me when I grow old..."

"Come off it! You don't have a son to marry her to. Now if she likes her men a little older, then I'd –"

"A *little* older? You're almost old enough to be her father yourself, Frank! And ugly to boot."

"It's not like we can all look like Prince Charming here," Frank muttered, gesturing towards Adrian.

Adrian chuckled in bemusement. "I'm too lowly and dishonest to be a prince."

Gerold slapped him on the back amiably. "You've got that right! Though anyone that falls for all those spells and potions of yours *deserves* to be conned."

"Most of them work, to be fair...if they were sold at the correct concentration," Adrian replied in an undertone.

"Oh, you're right. You're too sly to be Prince Charming. Best keep you well away from our Miss Scarlett."

"Keep who away from me?"

All three men turned in surprise to see who had spoken.

Of course it was Scarlett, but not a Scarlett whom Adrian had seen before, though he recognised her red dress immediately. This wasn't the girl with fear in her eyes, her feet bleeding and hair a tangled, wild mess as she fled the howling of the wolves.

No. This was a woman with gently curling, shining black hair framing her pale, heart-shaped face with the hint of a smile playing across her red, red lips. A crimson, fur-lined cloak cascaded down her shoulders, lending her the regal air of a queen. Her beauty had an unearthly quality to it that Adrian didn't quite understand, but it was clear that it wasn't just he who was enraptured by her.

Her smile disappeared when Scarlett realised that she had come face to face with Adrian. Her heavy lashes fluttered wide for a moment as she took a breath, then the smile reappeared, though it was altogether more formal.

"Mr Wolfe," she said, inclining her head slightly before turning to Frank. "Now what were you saying about me?"

"Miss Scarlett, happy birthday! You look breathtaking today."

She had the good sense to blush at the comment, though it was clear that Frank was trying to distract her. She glanced at Gerold. "Mr Rogers, my grandmother could do with some of that blue dye you said you were developing a few months ago. Do you have any?"

The man beamed as he slung an arm around Scarlett's shoulders and redirected her to his stall. "Anything for Old Lady Duke! As it happens, I made sure to bring extra just for her..."

Adrian turned back to his own stall to take note of what he was running low on. The long winter had depleted his stock of several herbs that should already be ripe for the picking, but were late to grow. He wondered if Heidi Duke had any, though he was loathe to ask.

After all, Adrian Wolfe detested the old woman down to his very soul, if indeed he had any soul left to hate a person with.

He glanced at Scarlett out of the corner of his eye, resplendent and glowing in red. When he had come across the young woman in the forest he had almost left her alone to die, simply to spite her grandmother. But Adrian was not a cold-blooded killer, and Scarlett held no responsibility for what Heidi had done to cause Adrian to hate her so much.

But now, looking at the woman's beloved grand-daughter, he had an idea.

When Scarlett had finished at Gerold's stall Adrian indicated for her to come over to his. In front of so many people she had no choice but to do as he wished, though she looked very much as if she wanted to run away.

He pretended to discuss a potion or two with her until both Gerold and Frank turned their attention to their other customers, then, when she was close enough to hear his voice, murmured, "You still haven't thanked me for saving your life, little miss."

Scarlett flinched. "You...disappeared."

"You saw me at the market just one month later."

"No I didn't."

"Liar."

She blushed furiously. "I didn't know what to say to you."

"What's so hard about 'thank you'?"

Scarlett hesitated. "...thank you."

"See, that wasn't difficult," he grinned, thoroughly enjoying the expression on Scarlett's face as he teased her. "What were you doing in the woods so late back then, anyway? And unsupervised! You could have run into *anyone*. Good thing I'm a gentleman."

"I highly doubt that," Scarlett bit out seemingly before she could stop herself, then covered her mouth with her hand as she realised what she'd just said.

"I highly doubt it, too," Adrian laughed, amused by her accidental candour, "though I must admit it stings to hear that from a young lady I most certainly *was* a gentleman to."

Scarlett's eyes darted up to his own and away again so quickly that Adrian almost imagined the action. "Really, thank you," she mumbled as she looked at her feet. "I didn't mean to insult you. I probably wouldn't be alive if not for you."

Oh, this is going to be fun, Adrian thought as he hooked a leather-gloved finger beneath Scarlett's chin and tilted her face up, only for her cheeks to burn in response. "No insult taken," he smiled. "Just so long as you stop so very clearly trying to ignore me from now on."

"I –"

But Scarlett didn't finish her sentence, instead breaking away from Adrian's touch in order to rush away towards the bakery across the street. A slew of people watched as her red cloak fluttered behind her, particularly the men, who couldn't take their eyes off her.

"Prince Charming, indeed," Gerold scoffed. "You've only gone and scared her off!"

Adrian shrugged. "I like a challenge."

"Don't you dare hurt Miss Scarlett's feelings."

"He'd have to be in with a chance with her to do that," Frank joked. "I have it on good authority that the baker's son's had his eyes on her for years."

"I thought it was the blacksmith? And Birch's boy?"

"So I have competition, it seems," Adrian murmured, not at all surprised. He knew the Dukes were the wealthiest family in town; it was natural that many of the single men in Rowan would be vying for Scarlett's affections. But she clearly wasn't used to the attention, given how she ran from Adrian merely touching her face. He had a sneaking suspicion that her confident, grown-up facade had been entirely her grandmother's doing.

That only works in my favour, Adrian thought wickedly as he spun a bottle full of turquoise liquid up into the air and expertly caught it to the delight and surprise of the group of young women currently passing by his stall. The liquid bubbled and fizzed for a few seconds and, once it had settled, the colour changed to a deep, inky purple. One of the women squealed in interest.

Women are so easy, Adrian thought with a grin as he sold the overly-diluted, useless potion to her as an attraction spell.

"I guess Miss Scarlett will be breaking several hearts over the next few weeks!" Gerold commented over on Adrian's left, the older man's eyes following the baker's son as he in turn followed Scarlett into his father's shop.

Adrian could only smirk. For whilst Scarlett broke the hearts of the simple boys in Rowan, he would work away at winning hers. It would be something Heidi Duke would be unable to abide. She'd beg for him to leave her precious grand-daughter alone.

And then, maybe then, Adrian could finally get back what she stole from him.

Yes, Scarlett's heart was the perfect bargaining chip. All Adrian had to do was make the shy, naive girl fall for him.

Something told him that it wouldn't be difficult at all.

CHAPTER THREE

Scarlett

"Miss Scarlett, might I – ah – have a word with you?"

Scarlett turned in surprise, her grandmother's cloak twirling around her as she did so. It was the baker's eldest son, Charlie. She gave him a gentle smile that belied the fact her heart was still battering in her ribcage after her unexpected encounter with Adrian Wolfe.

"Of course, Charlie. Is it alright if I finish paying your father first, though?"

Charlie's face grew red as a beet when he realised he

had interrupted the transaction, though his father merely laughed.

"Overeager as usual, my boy. I've put in a few extra buns for your birthday, Scarlett. Please wish Heidi well."

"Thank you kindly!" she beamed, before taking her basket now laden with baked goods from the counter and dutifully following Charlie back outside. He motioned towards the bench that sat outside the shop window, which an hour ago had been covered in frost. Now the sun had melted it away, leaving the grain of the carved wood littered with tiny droplets of water.

"Ah, let me dry that for you," Charlie said hurriedly, grabbing the cleaning rag he kept tucked underneath his belt and wiping away the moisture.

Scarlett motioned for him to stop before sitting down. "I'm fine, Charlie. My cloak will do more than a good enough job of keeping me dry."

He stared at the furred hood in barely-concealed envy. Scarlett had known the garment was expensive the moment she'd laid eyes on it, but she had grown up with expensive clothes all her life. She'd forgotten how such things looked to the other townspeople of Rowan.

"It's a hand-me-down," Scarlett found herself explaining, though in reality she had no need to defend herself for owning such a cloak. "My grandmother's. She gave me it today for my birthday."

"It's beautiful," Charlie replied, still eyeing the fur.

"Is that – wolf fur – by any chance?"

"It is, actually," she replied in surprise. "How did you know? I had no idea until Nana told me."

Charlie held up his hand, waiting for permission to touch the cloak, so Scarlett gave the barest of nods before the young man gently ran his fingers over the soft, luxurious fur. "I used to go out hunting with my Da when he was a little younger. Not so much anymore. I was always surprised by how soft the underfur was on a wolf. But usually the ones we caught weren't in the best shape so their fur was pretty useless. Not like this."

Despite the fact that the wolves had nearly killed Scarlett she somehow found herself not liking the idea of Charlie and his father venturing into the forest with the intention of hunting them down. It didn't seem...right, somehow.

"Nana said she's had this cloak since before she got married, so she must have taken especially good care of it for the fur to still be so soft," Scarlett murmured as she ran her fingers through it, then paused when Charlie's hand met hers. She glanced up through her lashes and saw that his face had grown red again, but it was resolute and determined.

"You're going to ask me to marry you, aren't you, Charlie?" she asked before she could stop herself. Scarlett had never been so bold before; clearly turning eighteen had allowed her to finally speak her mind.

Charlie looked taken aback by the question, though he kept his fingers intertwined through Scarlett's in the fur of her cloak. "I - yes. I was. I know I don't have much, but my father's bakery does well enough. But you would know that, since you're here most every day. And we have more than enough space in the house for you until we get a place of our own - which wouldn't be long because I've been saving, and -"

"Charlie, stop for a moment, please."

He looked at Scarlett in earnest, his blonde hair and freckled face dusted with flour.

Scarlett sighed. "Charlie, I'm not in line to inherit any of the Duke money. It's all going to my brothers."

"I...thought as much," he sighed, looking a little downcast. "I mean, why else would you be sent away from your father's house?"

"It's complicated. Let's just leave it at that."

But then Charlie grinned, his enthusiasm renewed. "I don't care about you not getting any of his money, Scarlett. You're the only girl in this whole town that I want to marry. You're well-spoken and pretty and helpful and my parents *love* you -"

"Miss Scarlett?"

Both Charlie and Scarlett frowned at each other at the interruption. They looked up in unison to see Jakob Schmidt, the blacksmith, standing in front of them, a very pretty bundle of snowdrops held between his burly hands.

Jakob was older than Scarlett by nearly ten years, and she had known him since she was very small. He dealt with all of her father's horses and so was often on the Duke property. Every spring he would gift Scarlett with a single snowdrop, which seemed so at odds with his rough demeanour that Scarlett at first found it amusing. But when she had reached twelve or so she had found the gesture very romantic and had even imagined herself marrying the man.

She couldn't imagine doing so now, though he was sweet, funny and hard-working. Which meant that Scarlett could only try her best to conceal her horror at the fact that Jakob might very well be intending to ask her the exact same question Charlie Beck had only just fumbled through.

"We were in the middle of something, Mr Schmidt," Charlie said, barely concealing his annoyance.

The older man shrugged. "Which was exactly why I interrupted. Can't have you jumping in before me, Beck." Jakob handed Scarlett the flowers, which she numbly accepted. "Miss Scarlett," he began as if Charlie wasn't there at all, "I have made no secret of my affection for you over the years. And now that you have grown into such a beautiful woman –"

Jakob paused, taking in Scarlett's appearance with deliberation, his eyes slightly wide as he realised how different she looked today. He took Scarlett's hands and motioned for her to stand up. Scarlett did so, feeling her face flush as Jakob took all of her in, focusing half a second too long on the curves of her breasts that could just barely be seen through the gap in her cloak. To her side Charlie also stood up, outraged into silence at Jakob's bold and blatant hijacking of his proposal.

"Beautiful doesn't even cover it," Jakob murmured. "Miss Scarlett, you are possibly the most lovely woman I have ever had the privilege of setting my eyes upon. You would honour me beyond belief in becoming my wife."

For a moment Scarlett didn't know what to say. It was easy to become swayed by Jakob's unexpectedly poetic words, especially after the over-eager, bumbling proposal Charlie had been in the middle of giving.

But then Scarlett cleared her throat and said, "Mr Schmidt, I shall say the same thing I said to Charlie – I do not stand to inherit any of my father's money."

Jakob merely waved a dismissive hand. "I do well enough. I don't care for your father's money – except what he spends on my services directly. Surely you must have known I'd intended to ask for your hand today, Scarlett?"

She shook her head. "I must profess to knowing nothing."

"Oh, your father is a crafty one," he laughed. "He was always so over-protective."

Scarlett frowned, as did Charlie beside her who had no idea what was going on. "I don't understand, Mr. Schmidt. What are you trying to say?"

He squeezed her hands around the snowdrops he'd gifted her. "I asked your father to allow me to marry you two years ago, Scarlett. But he said you were too young, which of course was true. But now you're not, and I have no intention of losing you to anybody else."

"Ah – Miss Scarlett?"

"*She's busy!*" both Charlie and Jakob roared at the new-found interruption. For behind Jakob stood a young man Scarlett hadn't seen in four years.

Andreas Sommer, older brother of Scarlett's childhood friend Henrietta. Their father, Otto, was a prominent doctor in the area, and Andreas had been training as a physician abroad in order to take up his place when his father retired.

He had grown taller in his time away. Along with the high arch of his cheekbones, fine clothes and perfectly styled hair, he looked every inch the kind of man Scarlett imagined her father would have wanted her to marry. In any other situation Scarlett would have been very happy to see him after four years apart.

But not today.

"I – Andreas – I did not know you had returned," she said simply.

Jakob and Charlie glared at their new rival, but Andreas seemed immune to them. He smiled dashingly for Scarlett.

"It has been too long, Scarlett. Might I speak to you in private?"

"You may not!" Charlie exclaimed. "*I* was speaking to her before the both of you interrupted!"

"Oh please, boy," Jakob said, all his previously poetic words forgotten. "You were barely managing to vocalise your thoughts before –"

"I was doing just fine!"

Scarlett's eyes darted between all three of them, feeling very much like a cornered animal.

"Scarlett," Andreas continued on in earnest, "when we were children our fathers had plans to betroth us, but for whatever unfortunate reason this never came to be more than a discussion."

Now I know exactly *why that never came to be,* Scarlett mused, thinking of Frances and how distressed she must have been by such a betrothal. She felt a keening sense of regret; marrying Andreas seemed very much like the path Scarlett was *supposed* to have taken before she was kicked out. It was the right proposal for her, rather than her adolescent fancy for the blacksmith who gave her snowdrops.

"Well you've missed your chance, Andreas," Jakob

said, surreptitiously trying to elbow the other man out of the way.

Behind them all Scarlett heard someone laughing raucously. For some reason she didn't need to see who it was to know that it was Adrian Wolfe. It made her feel angry. It made her feel small.

But above all, it dried up the last vestige of patience she had.

"Charlie, Mr Schmidt, Andreas – you must all realise your behaviour right now is entirely inappropriate," Scarlett said loudly, ensuring that many bystanders could hear her and help her escape if need be. The three men looked at her in surprise, perhaps shocked to realise that Scarlett was capable of raising her voice.

"Today is my birthday, and I came into town to fetch supplies to celebrate with my grandmother – not to listen to your proposals. Perhaps all three of you should take some time to rethink what it is you wish to say to me, and when it would actually be appropriate to say it. And perhaps..."

She rearranged her cloak over her shoulders, ran a hand through her hair and broke away from the three men, before turning back to look at them with a hint of a smile on her face.

"Perhaps you could all do with learning some manners. I'm a woman, not a horse up for auction. If you think I'd consider marrying *any* of you the way you are now, you are sadly mistaken."

And then she walked away with confidence, though it was all an act. In reality she was desperate to run away as fast as her legs could carry her, but that would only encourage them to run after her. No, she had to be strong and witty and opinionated, and maybe then they'd leave her be. She brought the snowdrops Jakob had given her up to her nose and smelled their crisp, gentle scent. She was allowed to keep them, even if she refused the man's proposal. They were a gift, after all, and she liked them.

When she walked by Adrian Wolfe and the rest of the travelling merchants she resisted the urge to look at her feet. Instead, she locked eyes with the man and nodded. His mouth quirked into a smile, the laughter from before still playing across his lips. Scarlett felt a heat coiling up inside her in response. It was like a snake, writhing around just below her stomach. She hadn't felt anything like it since the night he had saved her from the wolves. She had always thought it was because she was scared.

But she wasn't scared now, which meant it couldn't be because of fear.

She wasn't sure she wanted to know what it meant.

But, for now, Scarlett was going to return to her grandmother's and eat cake and regale her with the three disastrous proposals that had landed in her lap.

She could think about Mr Wolfe another day.

CHAPTER FOUR

Adrian

Adrian wasn't often in the town of Rowan just prior to the full moon. It involved him having to actually pay for room and board, which he had grown used to not paying whenever he was through. It was just about the only perk to what Heidi Duke had done to him.

"Sam, I don't know if you have a chance with her. She pretty much turned me down flat. Although it might have gone better if I hadn't been interrupted..."

Adrian had to resist the urge to laugh from his corner

table in the local tavern. Charlie Beck, the baker's son, was drowning his sorrows in beer with the miller's son – the one Adrian knew worked for Heidi on occasion. He'd seen him help Scarlett with her shopping before, too.

From a stool by the bar the blacksmith choked on his drink. "You never stood a shadow of a chance, Beck! Now I, on the other hand, was actually getting somewhere before Prince Childhood Friend showed up."

But his friend, whom Adrian didn't recognise, shook his head. "Come off it, Jakob. You really think she would have accepted *your* hand when she could marry Otto's boy?"

"See, Sam, you don't stand a chance," Charlie said once more.

Sam stayed silent, fiddling with his tankard with large, clumsy fingers. "She *might* say yes to me, Charlie...I'm with her almost every day."

"And has she ever shown any romantic inclination towards you, boy?" Jakob hollered over.

Sam's ears seemed to burn as he shook his head slightly, but then he stared at the blacksmith in earnest. "But Scarlett hasn't shown *anyone* affection, has she? So maybe she's just really good at keeping her feelings to herself."

Adrian had to hand it to the boy; clearly he didn't want to give up. Well, it wasn't as if he'd built up the courage to propose to Scarlett Duke yet. For all Adrian knew she *would* accept his hand in marriage.

But I can't let that happen, he thought, immediately much more interested in the conversation the men were having. *I can't let Scarlett accept* any *of their proposals.* For if she did then Adrian wouldn't be able to use her to lift his damned curse.

"She's always been happy to accept flowers from me," Jakob said almost haughtily. "And at least I already know how to treat a woman right. The two of you are still wet behind the ears."

"And what about me?"

Andreas glided into the tavern and interrupted the conversation as easily as he had interrupted Jakob's proposal. The older man rolled his eyes.

"I guess being a childhood friend counts for something," Charlie muttered reluctantly, "though Miss Scarlett wasn't exactly jumping straight into your arms, either."

The barkeep handed Andreas a tankard of ale and he sat himself down – unexpectedly – by Charlie and Sam, who both seemed rather surprised by the action.

"Where else do you expect me to sit?" Andreas asked, unperturbed. "I've been away for four years. Most of my friends are still abroad. How old are the two of you now, anyway?"

"Nineteen," Charlie replied defensively. "You're not going to spout all that 'wet behind the ears' nonsense too are you, Sommer? You're barely three years older than us."

Andreas chuckled. "Three years older but with a wealth of experience abroad. And I've known Scarlett since we were children. I'd say that puts me ahead of the two of you."

"Not ahead of Sam," Charlie said, willingly sacrificing his own claim in order to defend his friend against their rival. "He really does spend every day with Miss Scarlett. He's even seen her naked."

"*Charlie I told you that in private*," Sam growled through gritted teeth in a monotone that barely hid his horror at being called out.

The comment garnered the attention of most all the men in the tavern, particularly Jakob, who moved from the bar to squeeze in at the same table as his rivals. Even Gerold and Frank, who were sitting close to Adrian, moved their stools closer to listen into the conversation.

Of course Adrian was interested in what the boy had seen, but it wouldn't do to have everyone *know* that he was interested. He needed to keep a low profile and swoop in on Scarlett when the other men were all too busy trying to one-up each other. So he crossed his leather-clad legs, leaned back against the window and took a long draught of his beer, keeping his eyes half-closed as if he were sleeping, and listened carefully.

"You know, the past couple years she's clearly been trying to cover herself up but today she was dressed differently," Jakob said. "Now, that new cloak of hers was hiding most of her but my eyes don't lie – she's got some breasts on her, doesn't she, boy?"

Sam looked wildly discomfited by the question. But there were too many eyes on him, and the pressure was on. Something told Adrian he was incapable of lying.

"...yes," he mumbled. "They're, um, pretty perfect, like the rest of her."

"Outrageous!" Jakob protested, slamming his tankard down on the table to emphasise the word. "How is it that the miller's boy gets to see her naked *by accident* before me or even childhood friend over here? I'm beyond jealous."

"She was only fourteen when I left," Andreas murmured. "It wouldn't have been right for me to see her unclothed before now."

"Ah, I can't wait for the weather to get warmer," Charlie sighed wistfully. "We might see more of her, then. Has anyone seen Miss Scarlett swim in the lake or the river before?"

Even Sam shook his head. "She's fairly private."

"Do any of us even stand a chance? Miss Scarlett was pretty angry when she walked away this morning."

"Maybe you lads need some of Wolfe's love

potions," Gerold suddenly chimed in. Adrian opened his eyes wide at the comment, throwing a proverbial dagger the man's way as all attention was suddenly on him.

Charlie moved over to his table eagerly. "Do you really have something that would help, Mr Wolfe?! Do you?"

Adrian quirked an eyebrow. "I do. I won't sell you it, though."

"And why not?!"

"I think the little miss should be allowed to make her own choice, should she not?"

"But that shouldn't matter to you. I want to buy your potion, Mr Wolfe."

He crossed his arms and kept up as serious a face as possible. "Absolutely not. You couldn't afford it, anyway."

Charlie's shoulders fell. "I guess not. I bet Andreas could, though."

"Love potions are nonsense."

Adrian couldn't help but laugh. "Think that at your own risk, doctor. I suppose it would make it all the more satisfying to watch you fall under the effects of one of them." He was thinking of the young woman he had sold the attraction potion to earlier that day, who had professed to having an eye on the man now that he was back. It was far too weak to work *properly,* but the look on Andreas' face as Adrian's words sunk in was priceless.

Jakob laughed loudly as he thumped Andreas on the back. "That's what you get for insulting a merchant, Sommer. But I guess we should all just listen to what Scarlett actually said rather than trying to bewitch her."

Sam frowned. "What did she say?"

None of them expected Adrian to answer. "To paraphrase: don't corner her on the street and profess your undying love in front of the whole town one after the other and then get into a pissing contest that doesn't actually put her feelings into consideration whatsoever. Oh, and perhaps be a little more romantic."

The three men who had proposed to Scarlett had the sense to look abashed.

"I guess we *did* look like idiots," Jakob admitted.

"And now Sam has the advantage," Charlie said. "He can perfect his first proposal and not look like a damn fool."

I can't be having that, Adrian thought. He rummaged through the pockets in his cloak, where he stored small bottles of very concentrated potions that, for once, actually did what they were supposed to do. Locating the vial in question, which was half-full of colourless liquid, Adrian finished his beer, stood up and nodded good-bye to the men he'd been forced into conversation with.

When he moved past their table he slipped some of

the vial's contents into Sam's tankard. Not a single person noticed.

"I'll have to speak to my father about organising a meeting with Mr Duke," Adrian heard Andreas say as he crossed the tavern floor for the stairs up to the bedrooms on the first floor.

"But she's been disinherited for some reason," Charlie said.

"Doesn't mean proper decorum shouldn't be followed."

"Show off..."

Adrian climbed the rickety stairs in silence up to his room. The substance he'd slipped Samuel Birch would cause him to forget about proposing to Scarlett for three days. That gave him three days to woo and impress Scarlett enough that she'd never consider accepting the boy's affections. By most anyone's standards that was barely any time at all. For Adrian, who wouldn't be able to do anything once the full moon rose, it was even less.

But that didn't matter. He would do it.

Three days was all Adrian Wolfe needed.

CHAPTER FIVE

Scarlett

"Nana, where's the sugar?"

"Where it always is, Red."

"It's not in the cupboard," Scarlett said in exasperation. "Where did you put it?"

"Oh, Miss Scarlett, that's my fault," Sam murmured from the parlour, where he was building a fire in preparation for the sun setting. He came through to the kitchen and reached up to one of the higher shelves that Scarlett couldn't reach and pulled down the jar of sugar she'd been looking for. "I was helping your grandmother tidy up yesterday and put it on the shelf."

Scarlett smiled warmly. "Thank you, Sam."

"No problem."

Sam scratched his head, then, and wrinkled his nose as if a fly had landed on it. It made Scarlett giggle.

"What's wrong, Sam?" she asked. "Seems like something's on your mind."

"There's nothing wrong. Well, at least I don't *think* there's something on my mind," he muttered as he fiddled with the ochre braces holding his trousers up.

"How can you not know whether something's on your mind or not?"

"He's probably hungover, the rate he was drinking last night."

Scarlett turned; by the open front door stood a grinning Adrian Wolfe. Her heart felt like it had jumped into her throat quite suddenly, which she didn't like in the slightest.

"Knock, knock," he chuckled, silently chapping his knuckles against the door.

"What are you doing here so late?" Scarlett's grandmother complained as she got up from the table, where she'd been knitting. "It's almost sunset! We were just about to retire to the parlour before the wolves started up their *dreadful* howling."

Adrian seemed amused by the comment, though Scarlett failed to see what was so funny.

"I was wondering if you still kept a stock of tansy and sweet violet?" he asked. "I'm all out."

Her grandmother frowned. "And why should I give any of it to you?"

"Because I'll pay?"

She sighed heavily; for a long moment Scarlett was sure she would refuse, though she had no idea why her grandmother and Adrian Wolfe were on such bad terms. Scarlett had always thought her grandmother would be grateful to the man for saving her life.

But now, thinking about it, hadn't Nana initially been angry that Adrian was outside her house in the first place two years ago?

Now all Scarlett could wonder about was what Adrian had done to anger her grandmother so.

Eventually the old woman nodded and, with some reluctance, got up from her chair and beckoned for Sam to help her. "I keep my stocks in the attic these days. Come on, Samuel, I need you to pull the ladder down for me."

Sam looked very much like he didn't want to leave Scarlett alone in the kitchen with a man she barely knew, but then he frowned as if in confusion and ran a hand through his hair. He shook his head as he followed Scarlett's grandmother through to the corridor.

There were a few seconds of awkward silence as Scarlett moved about the kitchen making tea. She was very aware that Adrian's unsettling eyes followed her wherever she went.

"So where's the cloak, Red?"

She flinched. "Don't call me that."

"But that's what Heidi calls you. And it's what your name means."

"Even so."

"Red it is, then," he said, smirking when Scarlett finally looked away from her tea to glare at him.

"What were you talking about when you said Sam was hungover?"

Adrian moved from the doorway to settle into a chair before Scarlett could say anything about it, stretching out his long legs in front of him in satisfaction. He was dressed in black as usual, though the braces that held up the dark leggings largely hidden by his leather boots were silver. They matched the strange, white streak in his hair.

He shrugged. "He was drinking a lot in the tavern with those men who asked to marry you yesterday."

Scarlett bristled, turning away from Adrian in order to curl her hands into the wooden counter-top by the wash basin. The more she thought about what had happened the more annoyed she became, especially because Adrian had witnessed the entire thing.

"They were all talking about you," he continued jovially. "Apparently your Mr Birch has seen you naked before."

"He *what?*" Scarlett exclaimed, outraged and mortified. Her eyes darted to the corridor and back again to confirm that both Sam and her grandmother were out of earshot, then rounded on Adrian lounging by the kitchen table as if he owned the place. She narrowed her eyes. "You're only saying that to tease me."

"Oh, that's definitely so, but that doesn't mean it isn't true. They were all very enthusiastically discussing how you – ah – *measured up*, as it were. Now that I can see you without the cloak on I can ascertain that Samuel was telling the truth. Maybe you should wear a little more when he's around just so he doesn't get any ideas...or so your lack of attire doesn't excite unexpected guests."

Scarlett had no idea what Adrian was talking about at first, then felt her cheeks flush as she glanced downward. She was wearing the white smock she tended to wear to bed, though it was several years old and much too small for her now. The bodice barely held in her breasts and the skirt skimmed a few inches above her knees, something which Scarlett had never deemed an issue before given that nobody came out to visit her grandmother unexpectedly. And Sam was, well, Sam.

61

Clearly I need to rethink that last part, Scarlett thought, *though if he's already seen me naked then there's nothing else new for him to see.*

Shocked by her own obvious lack of modesty, she looked about for something to cover herself up.

Adrian merely laughed. "Good; be more aware of yourself. Never mind those wolves two years ago – a baker, a blacksmith and a doctor almost ate you whole yesterday morning. That sounds like the beginning of a joke."

"Do you take *nothing* seriously?"

Adrian stared at her. Scarlett had to fight the instinct to look away.

"Maybe. Maybe not. Why, are you interested?"

"No."

"Liar."

"Stop calling me a liar."

"I will when you stop lying."

"Who are you to tell me what to do?"

Adrian stood up and closed the gap between them, brushing a gloved hand against Scarlett's chin where he had touched her the day before. She couldn't believe he had the audacity to do such a thing in her grandmother's house.

"An interested party," he murmured, gently turning Scarlett's head left and right with his hand. She numbly allowed him to. "You really have grown up, little miss. Though I did enjoy the frightened look on your face when you were sixteen."

Disconcertingly close, a wolf howled, and Scarlett's eyes widened as her body twitched and her heart raced with the memory of the very night Adrian was talking about.

"Ah – that one. Beautiful."

He watched Scarlett intently, his amber eyes fiery in the bleeding light that filtered through the window as the sun began to die. The white in his hair flashed gold when he cocked his head to the side as if he were anticipating what Scarlett would do next.

The action didn't seem entirely human. Scarlett didn't know why.

"You're...very strange, Mr Wolfe."

It was an understatement, but it was all Scarlett could think to say without very obviously insulting the man. And then he grinned, drawing back his thin lips to reveal sharp, white canines. He moved away from Scarlett, retreating to the front door just as her grandmother and Sam returned to the kitchen.

"I found what you needed, Adrian," her grandmother said as she handed him a small, paper-wrapped packet, "but it could do with drying out by a fire. Be sure to do so before you use them for anything."

"Naturally. Many thanks, Heidi."

And then he was gone as quickly as he'd disappeared the night he'd saved Scarlett's life.

"Miss Scarlett?" Sam wondered aloud. "Are you okay?"

"Hmm?"

She turned to face Sam, though she barely saw him. Her hand had found its way to her chin, where Adrian had touched her. Part of her wished he hadn't been wearing gloves. Part of her was very, sincerely glad he had.

And then she came back to her senses and remembered what Adrian had said about Sam.

"I'm going to get changed. I'm cold," she muttered suddenly before rushing out of the kitchen.

In reality she was burning.

CHAPTER SIX

Adrian

Heidi Duke wasn't aware anyone was watching her. And, for all intents and purposes, nobody was. Unless one counted the animals, in which case there was a solitary pair of amber eyes shadowing her every move through the window.

Adrian prowled on silent paws, making sure not to be seen by the old woman responsible for his affliction. She seemed blissfully unaware of his presence, which was just as well. If she noticed then he'd likely suffer an even deeper curse than the one she had cast on him six years ago.

Because for the three nights surrounding the full moon, each and every month of the year, Adrian's surname was *exactly* what he became.

And for selling the wretched woman fake potions, no less. Talk about grudges.

Adrian had been a fresh-faced twenty-year-old merchant at the time, setting off on his own after a plague had wiped out much of the village he had hailed from, including his parents. His father had been a professional con-man, whilst his mother was a healer. They'd always joked that opposites attract, and had been sickeningly in love for all of Adrian's life. The cumulative knowledge passed down from them to him had resulted in their son arrogantly assuming he could pass off diluted potions and spells even as he sold legitimate remedies for genuine ailments.

That had worked...for a while. It was, for the most part, fanciful, flighty young women who bought his potions, anyway. Nobody expected them to actually *work*. He made them just strong enough for the person who bought them to fleetingly capture the attention of their target before wearing off entirely. For most of them this was all they really desired – a fantasy.

Heidi Duke was not one of those young, flighty women. No, she had required something much stronger from him. Much darker. A poison of the soul, that slowly clawed away at the very edges of a person until there was nothing left inside of them. Adrian *had* possessed what she wanted to purchase.

He just hadn't wanted to give it away.

And so he'd sold the woman a version of the poison so weak that its effects were non-existent.

What he hadn't expected was for her to knock him over the head, tie him to a tree and feed him his own poison, thus demonstrating that Adrian had been trying to con her out of her money.

Heidi had been furious. Adrian was sure he was going to die, that day. It seemed as if she intended to keep him tied there at the mercy of the wolves. But then those wolves had given her an idea, and Heidi cruelly bewitched Adrian to turn into one of the very creatures that roamed the forest.

It was supposed to teach him a lesson. It was supposed to force Adrian to stop conning innocent townspeople with his diluted potions and feather-weak spells.

Adrian Wolfe, being Adrian Wolfe, had learned no such lesson, though he made sure to never sell Heidi Duke anything other than exactly what she asked for from then on. This seemed to sufficiently satisfy the woman, much to Adrian's relief.

To this day the two of them kept up some semblance of a truce, where the two of them traded and bartered and sold to each other as and when needed, but otherwise kept to their own devices. Adrian had been content with this for a while, but no more.

He wanted his whole life back.

Being a wolf was dangerous. He had to avoid other packs who viewed him as a threat. He had to avoid humans who would kill him if they could. To that end he couldn't risk travelling anywhere that wolves didn't exist when he was due to change. There would be nowhere to hide.

It was terrifying and stressful and, above all, limiting. All he could do was return to the same woods every month where the regular wolves just barely now accepted his presence.

He wanted free of it all. But for that he needed something so important to Heidi Duke that she'd have no choice but to revoke the curse she'd placed upon Adrian.

He needed Scarlett.

Adrian was fairly certain the young woman had no idea what her precious *Nana* was capable of; he reasoned that nobody was.

If they only knew what she was doing when everyone was asleep at night, he thought as he dared stalk a little closer to the light pouring out of the kitchen window. Heidi was reading a book and preparing herbs. It was so innocuous that even if her precious grand-daughter or Samuel Birch were to suddenly appear they would have no idea what the old woman was doing.

But Adrian knew.

Atropa belladonna. Opium poppy. Water hemlock from the Americas. They were all on the table. But it wasn't poisonous plants that Adrian most feared her for. Anybody could poison a person if they got their hands on the plants and processed them correctly.

No, it was her curses. They were far stronger than anything Adrian had learned of or had indeed constructed himself. He'd seen his fair share of people afflicted by curses who had sought his mother for aid and yet, even still, Heidi's curses were stronger. It unnerved him to no end. Deep, deep down inside his heart, where nobody could see, Adrian knew she had to die.

She was too powerful to be walking the earth. The wolves seemed to innately understand this. They didn't dare come close to her accursed house. It was the only reason anybody could live out here in the first place.

Adrian wasn't even sure how old Heidi really was. She could be hundreds of years old for all anyone knew. Thousands.

Bored with watching the old woman through the limited colours his wolf eyes granted him, Adrian soundlessly padded his way around to the back of the house to the window overlooking Scarlett's bedroom. Dully he thought of Samuel Birch, and how it was through this very window that he must have spied the woman in a state of undress.

Scarlett wasn't asleep, as Adrian had expected. She was sitting up in bed with her back against the wall, clutching a pillow and...doing nothing. Thinking. Her face was red.

Stupidly – recklessly – Adrian prowled closer and closer to the window, bushy tail swinging softly behind him as he loped forwards. He needed only to reach up and place his front paws on the windowsill and his nose would hit the icy-cold glass separating him from the woman inside.

And so he did.

Scarlett was watching.

Adrian didn't dare move as she slowly edged towards him, which was the exact opposite of what a person was supposed to do when they saw a wolf outside their window. Perhaps it was because the glass was thick, and the fact that wolves didn't have the opposable thumbs required to unlock the latch, but Scarlett knelt in front of the window and pressed the very tip of her nose to the glass.

Her scent filled Adrian's nostrils through the smallest of cracks between the window and its frame, all vanilla and saffron and sandalwood. Even as a wolf it was enticing. As a man it might have driven him to break open the window and steal Scarlett into the darkness of the forest and do unspeakable things to her.

But Adrian wasn't a man right now. He could do nothing but stare at her winter-blue eyes, until eventually Scarlett's perfectly-formed lips parted.

"Knock, knock, Mr Wolf," she whispered, gently rapping her knuckles against the glass as she spoke, though her eyes were wide in terror at what she was doing.

Adrian fled.

He didn't stop until he could no longer see nor smell Heidi's Duke's house, and the young woman lying within it.

CHAPTER SEVEN

Scarlett

The list of supplies Scarlett's grandmother needed from town was much longer – and far more bizarre – than usual.

"What in the world does she need concentrated hemlock for?" Scarlett muttered aloud as she reached the market. She knew it was a poison, and a strong one at that. She hadn't noticed any vermin eating the plants in the garden that would need getting rid of. But she knew her grandmother was far more knowledgeable about the natural world around them than Scarlett ever could be.

She trusted that the old woman needed it for something Scarlett likely couldn't fathom.

A flash of copper hair at waist height caught her eye as she stopped by the fountain in the middle of the market square. For a moment Scarlett's spirits soared, thinking that it might be Rudy or Elias running rampant through the livestock auction, but a few seconds later she recognised the child as Charlie Beck's younger brother, David.

Scarlett's heart hurt at the sight of him. Maybe it was because of the slew of marriage proposals she had received causing her to think of her family but, whatever the reason, she wanted nothing more than to curl up by the fire in her father's study as she read a fairytale to her little brothers whilst her father finished with his accounting and her 'mother' fussed for her brothers to go to bed.

It will never be like that again, she thought sadly, just as little David ran full-pelt into Scarlett's skirt. She was dressed in dark grey beneath her red cloak, perhaps inspired by the wolf that had mysteriously appeared by her window the night before.

Scarlett nearly dropped her basket in surprise as the child extricated himself from her legs and looked up at her with a wide grin on his face. One of his front baby teeth had fallen out.

"Sorry, Miss Scarlett," he said, giggling when she ruffled his curly hair.

"I hope you're not causing your mother any mischief, little one."

"No..."

"David Beck, get back here this instant!" his mother, Brenda, bellowed across the crowd until she reached her son. She grimaced apologetically at Scarlett. "I'm so sorry about him. That's the last time I let him near the pastries for breakfast."

"Don't worry about it," Scarlett replied, smiling. "He's a charming boy."

"More charming than his older brother?"

It was Scarlett's turn to grimace. "I wasn't exactly in a position to respond to anything Charlie said properly."

Brenda snorted. "So I heard! You do right by yourself, Miss Scarlett. If my boy had any sense he'd have *prepared* for asking for your hand. Just know that I would consider it an honour and a gift from God to welcome you into the family. Heaven knows I could do with another woman around!"

"Thank you, Mrs Beck," Scarlett replied, genuinely moved by the woman's sentiments – especially considering she had only just been thinking miserably about her own, estranged family. "I *do* need to get going now, though. Nana gave me a long list to work through."

"Of course! Sorry about David being a nuisance again. Have a lovely day, Miss Scarlett!"

"And you."

Brenda dragged her youngest son along with her as he stared back longingly at Scarlett, whom he clearly thought he'd wrangled into playing with him.

Now in a somewhat better mood than she had been in, Scarlett swung her basket slightly as she made her rounds and collected the various supplies her grandmother needed. She was relieved not to run into Charlie, nor Jakob, nor Andreas, all three of whom Scarlett did not have the patience to deal with right now. Though she knew it was only pertinent to visit the Sommer family soon now that Andreas had returned – her father would be pleased by her doing so and Henrietta would no doubt be happy to see her.

My father hasn't even seen me to wish me a happy birthday, Scarlett thought, unbidden, and she began to feel miserable again. So she forced herself to think about another matter. Anything would do.

Invariably she thought of the wolf.

Why had it come so close to the window? No wolves ever dared to step foot within the small clearing that enclosed her grandmother's house. Why had it watched her for so long? And why had *she* approached it?

She thought of its eyes, but then of course she thought of another wolf by name. For Adrian's eyes really were akin to a wolf's, as unlikely as it may have seemed. Considering the unnatural white streak in his hair, and the fact he sold potions and spells, Scarlett had to wonder whether he had taken something to change the colour of his irises for dramatic effect.

It was the only reasonable explanation she could come up with.

Nearly two hours later she had managed to purchase everything on her grandmother's list bar one item: the hemlock. The apothecary didn't stock it, neither did Rowan's two most prominent healers. Scarlett knew someone who would almost certainly have it, of course.

She simply didn't want to ask him for it.

But Scarlett didn't want to go back home without everything on the list and so, with some reluctance, she struggled over to Adrian Wolfe's stall, arms laden with her basket overflowing with everything else her grandmother had asked for.

Adrian's stall was swarming with the usual girls who fawned over the man and senselessly spent every coin they had on his ridiculous love potions and spells. Littered in amongst them were older folk looking for some of his far more respectable salves, which Scarlett knew from first-hand use actually worked when one was suffering from a fever or chills.

"Ex-excuse me," she mumbled as she tried to make her way though. When nobody moved, she called out in a firmer voice, "*Excuse me.*"

Finally some of the girls looked at her, distaste

apparent on their faces, before returning their attention to Adrian without moving an inch.

Scarlett began to yell profanities inside her head when she heard a familiar chuckle. "Come on, ladies, I know you aren't buying anything today. Let Miss Scarlett through before she drops everything she's carrying."

That seemed to do the trick, though the girls kept looking back with wistful glances at Adrian as they stalked away. Scarlett didn't care; apart from Henrietta, she had never been popular with the other Rowan girls. She'd always had nicer dresses than them, and faster horses than them, and better marriage prospects than them. Even when Scarlett had moved to her grandmother's house their opinion of her hadn't changed, and that suited Scarlett just fine even as she admitted to herself, back when she was sixteen, that she was lonely.

"What on earth have you bought, Red?" Adrian asked as he deftly lifted the basket out of Scarlett's arms and placed it on an empty space behind his stall for safekeeping. "And where is that miller's son when you need him?"

"Working for his father," Scarlett replied. "I need hemlock."

Adrian's eyebrow – the one that was cut in half by a scar – quirked at the request. "Straight to business today, it seems."

"What else would you expect from a customer?"

"Small talk, maybe. 'What is all this cold weather about?' or, 'Oh, Mr Wolfe, don't you look dashing today!'"

Scarlett rolled her eyes, though in truth Adrian *did* look dashing today. He was dressed in, of all colours, red – red braces and red leggings and a white shirt with his usual leather boots and gloves. Slung over his stall lay a matching red waistcoat. It made a startling difference from his usual black.

"Hello Mr Wolfe, you finally look like you haven't just come from a funeral. Happy?"

He threw his head back and laughed heartily at Scarlett's comment. It was annoyingly infectious; she found her lips curling into a smile despite herself.

"My favourite colour seems to be brushing off on you, too," Adrian said when he finished laughing, reaching out to just barely touch the grey fabric of Scarlett's dress that was peeking out from her cloak. "It seems as if we've swapped."

"I was in a grey mood."

"Oh? And what's a grey mood, I wonder?"

"Do you have hemlock or not?"

He sighed dramatically. "I know you're capable of much better small talk than that, Red. I've seen you talk to every other merchant in this square."

Scarlett stayed silent.

"Okay, okay, you win," Adrian finally said in resignation, before disappearing behind his stall to rummage around in a locked box. "How is Heidi wanting this? Leaves? Powder? Concentrated?"

"Concentrated."

"Of course."

Scarlett hesitated for a moment, then asked, "Do you know why she needs something so dangerous?"

For the first time since the man had saved her life, Adrian's face was stony and serious as he placed a small vial into a straw-lined box. "Ask her yourself, Scarlett."

Scarlett was taken aback by the abruptness of the comment. She'd expected a joke or a lie or – something. It made her feel uneasy.

But then Adrian smiled, and he carefully stowed away the little box inside Scarlett's already overflowing basket of goods. When some of the items at the top began to tumble and fall, he disappeared beneath his stall and retrieved another basket, filling it up until both baskets evenly contained everything Scarlett had come into town to buy.

"I – thank you," she murmured. "How much for the hemlock?"

"For Heidi, no charge."

Scarlett stared at him in surprise. "Really? Why?"

"She never charged me for those herbs yesterday. Tell her I consider us even."

She nodded. "Will do."

Then she took both baskets, hanging one off each arm, and headed off without another word. She was barely out of the market square on her way back to the woods, however, when she heard the sound of someone running after her. Thinking that it was Charlie, or Jakob, or even Andreas, she sighed heavily before turning to face whoever it was with the intention of telling them to leave her alone.

But it was Adrian.

CHAPTER EIGHT

Adrian

"I'd say you need some help with those baskets, Red."

"Get back to your stall, Mr Wolfe. You have customers who no doubt miss you."

He waved a hand dismissively. "That's one of the perks of being a merchant; I can take a break whenever I want. And Gerold is watching it, anyway."

Scarlett frowned as she turned her back on him and continued towards the woods. "Thanks, but no thanks. I can handle the baskets myself."

"I'm sure you can," Adrian said as he quickened his pace to catch up with her, "but that doesn't mean you wouldn't benefit from some help."

"Again: thanks but no thanks."

But then Adrian stepped in front of Scarlett and placed his hands on her shoulders to stop her. He put the most serious expression he could muster on his face. "You and I both know the wolves are in the woods right now. It's safer not to travel alone."

"I came in on my own."

"Yes, and that was foolish."

Scarlett hesitated. "It'll still be light for hours. I'll be fine."

He smiled. "Humour me."

Scarlett eyed him critically. Adrian had put his red waistcoat on before going after her, completing his outfit for her benefit, though he had no cloak or coat to speak of. From the look on Scarlett's face Adrian knew she was wondering how he wasn't cold.

"You don't look like you'd be much help against the wolves dressed like that."

But Scarlett had barely completed her sentence before he gracefully slid a concealed blade from his right boot, then indicated another attached to his waist. He flashed her a grin. "I'm not so unprepared, Red. And you know yourself how quickly I can move through these woods."

Finally she relented, if only because it was clear that Adrian would not give up. "Fine," she grumbled, "*fine.* Help me if you must," before dumping the heavier of her two baskets into his arms.

Adrian laughed. "No need to be so graceless about it. I'm merely concerned for your safety."

"You're only out for yourself, Mr Wolfe," Scarlett called out as she marched ahead.

"So what do you call me leaving my place of work to carry a basket for you?"

"Self-indulgence. You're getting a kick out of this. You enjoy teasing me, though Lord knows why."

"I told you why yesterday."

Scarlett briefly glanced at him out of the corner of her eye as the two of them reached the fringe of trees that marked the beginning of the woods. "And what did you tell me yesterday?"

"That I'm interested in you."

He watched her bite her lip slightly as her cheeks slowly flushed. Above them the sun filtered through the bare branches of the trees, alternately casting light then shadow across the two of them. The air grew colder as they moved deeper into the woods, though it was already unseasonably cold directly beneath the sun. If Adrian didn't know for a fact that it was early April he'd have sworn it was January.

"You have nothing to say in response?" he asked after a while, hanging back a few paces in order to watch Scarlett walk in from of him. A smile crossed his face as she neatly hopped up and over a creeping tree trunk that had grown across the path.

"I don't think it *warrants* a response. There's a difference."

"You responded to all of those proposals. What makes my interest any different?"

"You can't possibly believe that what Charlie, Jakob and Andreas said and what *you* said hold the same weight."

Adrian scoffed at her comment. "You never intended to marry any of them, anyway. Surely that means I actually have more of a chance than them?"

"And what made you arrive at that ridiculous conclusion?"

Adrian crept up silently behind Scarlett and slid an arm around her waist, snaking it beneath her cloak as she gasped in surprise.

"Because you don't react like this with anyone else," he murmured against her ear, tightening his grip a little on her waist as he did so.

"N-nobody dares touch me like this, that's why!"

"Maybe that's their problem. None of them are bold enough. *I* am, though."

"Clearly."

Adrian brushed his lips against Scarlett's neck, just above the fur of her cloak. Her skin was burning. "So is that a yes? Or a no?"

"...to what?"

"To whether I have a chance in hell with you."

Scarlett's eyes darted towards Adrian's for a moment. But when she tried to look away he let the basket he was holding drop in order to spin her around to face him. He ran a hand through Scarlett's hair and just barely brought her lips to his.

She was unfalteringly looking at him now, eyes wide and bright with the kind of fear brought about by being in an exciting, unfamiliar situation. Scarlett let the basket she was holding drop to the ground to join the other one, her hand now limp and useless at her side.

"Why did you do that?" she whispered in a wavering voice.

Adrian merely pressed his mouth against hers a little harder, biting down very gently on Scarlett's upper lip in the process. His hand on her waist slid around to the small of her back, urging her closer towards him little by little.

As if remembering that she had hands of her own, Scarlett raised her arms and splayed her fingers out across Adrian's chest. It seemed as if she was preparing to push him away but it never happened. Adrian could hear her heart thumping wildly; he was sure Scarlett could feel his own accelerated heart-rate against her palms.

"I seem to recall a meeting rather akin to this two years ago," Adrian said, voice low and silky as the words fell upon Scarlett's lips. "Your heart was like a drum back then, too."

Scarlett hardly seemed to dare to blink as Adrian kept his eyes on hers. "I was...terrified," she uttered.

"And now?"

"I think I am now, too."

He chuckled as he wound his hand further into Scarlett's hair. "Not necessarily a bad thing. Is that all you feel?"

"I – no."

"Excited?"

She just barely nodded.

"On fire?"

Her eyes closed for a moment. "...yes."

"See? That wasn't so hard to say."

She opened her eyes once more, frowning uncertainly. "What is it that you want from me?"

"Nothing not given willingly, Miss Scarlett."

And then, at the moment when it seemed as if she might finally kiss him back, Adrian pulled away from her. He bent down and reorganised the baskets, retrieving items that had rolled away before standing back up and placing both into Scarlett's arms.

"Your grandmother's house is only a few minutes away. I best be getting back to Rowan."

Scarlett watched him with a dazed expression on her face as if she couldn't quite believe what had just transpired. It was only after Adrian had turned from her and began to walk away that she shouted after him, in a querulous voice, "You're a sly one, Mr Wolfe!"

"So I've heard!" he called back, raising a hand in good-bye without looking back.

As he headed back into Rowan he felt like whooping.

Three days? Who ever thought I needed three days!

Adrian Wolfe needed only one.

CHAPTER NINE

Scarlett

"Little Red, oh little Red, time to wake up!"

"I'm already awake, Nana," Scarlett called back from her room. She was sitting in front of her mirror, carefully braiding her hair like a crown around her head. Though she was merely going to the market Scarlett wanted to look good. She knew it was because of Adrian Wolfe.

She hated that it was because of Adrian Wolfe.

To that end Scarlett had chosen to wear a low-cut, white blouse beneath a deep green dress; it fell to just below her knees and laced up tightly around the bodice, bringing in her waist and accentuating her breasts and hips. It was the first time she had knowingly dressed in such a manner.

Him seeing me in that too-small nightdress doesn't count, Scarlett thought, face flushing at the memory. It seemed as if she was doomed to be embarrassed by every encounter she had with the man. She knew it was because she lacked experience when it came to dealing with the opposite sex, whereas Adrian Wolfe had experience in abundance...if Scarlett used his manner when dealing with the women of Rowan as evidence.

It infuriated her that she still felt like that scared sixteen-year-old girl he had found running from the wolves in the woods. Scarlett had grown up, in more ways than one, and now that she was finally in a position to acknowledge that she had no idea what to do with herself.

I can't believe he kissed me. Twice! And then he walked away!

Scarlett was outraged by this. She felt very much as if Adrian was making fun of her, though he had professed to only doing so because he liked her. But he had waited for Scarlett to admit to being attracted to him before leaving, as if that was all he'd wanted to hear. Part of her was afraid that the man would lose interest in her now that she'd all but given in.

And so Scarlett was choosing to dress up as if to tell Adrian not to lose interest. It made Scarlett feel somewhat foolish, but she was going to do it anyway, even though there was no guarantee the merchant was even still in Rowan. He usually only stayed for three days – and he'd stayed for four already this month – so in all likelihood he really had already left.

Something told Scarlett this wasn't the case, however. She didn't know what.

Letting a few tendrils of hair loose from her braided crown to frame her face, and staining her lips the barest red, Scarlett for once chose to wear low-heeled, black leather shoes with a silver buckle instead of her usual boots.

When she moved through to the kitchen her grandmother smiled in approval.

"Now *that's* more like the Scarlett Duke I want the world to see," she said. "Samuel, be a dear and escort my grand-daughter to market."

Sam – who was once more visible only through the open window as he tended to the garden – nodded immediately as he brushed himself off. He was dressed better than usual, Scarlett noted, in olive trousers, dark braces and a white shirt that complimented his permanently tanned skin. Her heart accelerated slightly even as Scarlett admonished herself for getting excited at the mere sight of a handsome man.

It finally seemed as if the weather had taken a turn for the better, and for the first time all year the air no longer held the chill of winter. With the pleasant sunshine and the warmth of the new southerly wind, Scarlett shook her head when her grandmother handed her the red cloak.

"I think I'll go without today, Nana," she said as she stepped outside where Sam stood waiting for her. "It would cover my outfit, anyway."

"Good to see you're learning," she grinned. "Now all you need is for a good, strong man to offer you *his* cloak when you pretend to shiver."

Scarlett rolled her eyes before setting off through the woods with Sam. Most of their journey passed by in a flurry of polite, easy conversation – the type of conversation she had come to expect them to have once Sam got over his usual, initial shyness.

But as they got closer and closer to Rowan the young man became somewhat fidgety. Whilst they passed through the permanent twilight beneath the trees Sam kept stealing glances at Scarlett, growing red in the face when she noticed him looking. Eventually she could take it no more.

"Just what is it you're looking at, Sam?" she demanded when they were but five minutes from the market square of Rowan.

Sam seemed somewhat taken aback by the question. He shoved his hands into the pockets of his trousers and stared at the earth beneath their feet for a few moments in silence, as if intending not to answer her. But then their eyes locked onto each other, whilst a nervously earnest look crossed Sam's face that confused Scarlett to no end.

"Sam...?"

"You know when you asked me the other day, Miss Scarlett," he said quickly, "whether I had something on my mind, and I said I wasn't sure?"

"Um, yes?" Scarlett replied uncertainly, wondering where Sam was taking the conversation.

"Well, I – ah – I don't really *know* why I wasn't sure at the time – maybe I really was hungover like Mr Wolfe said – but I know, very clearly, what's on my mind now. It's been all I can think about for a long time, after all."

"Sam, where is this going?"

His face grew even redder than Scarlett's namesake. He gestured towards the large, ornate fountain in the centre of the market square. "Can we sit down over there to talk?"

Scarlett nodded and followed him over, feeling altogether overcome by the unsettling sensation of déjà-vu. She delicately perched on the edge of the fountain as flecks of water momentarily darkened the fabric of her dress, only to disappear a second or two later.

The sun was shining directly in Sam's face; he held up a hand to shield his eyes as he stared, unsmiling and nervous, at Scarlett. She abruptly felt like she wanted to run away, though she steeled herself to the spot for Sam's sake.

He sucked in a deep breath. "Miss Scarlett, we've known each other for two years now. I know that isn't the longest time in the world, but I feel like at this point we both know each other rather well."

She smiled slightly at this. It was true, of course, and it filled her with affection for the sandy-haired young man still getting used to how broad and tall he now was.

He continued. "I was there when you first came to live with your grandmother. I know how complicated things are with your family. I know how much you miss them. I know how much you want to be with them again...for things to go back to the way they were."

Scarlett felt the corners of her eyes begin to sting at Sam's words. She knew he didn't mean them unkindly but the reminder of what Scarlett had lost was still as bitter as it had always been.

"But you and I both know that something like that won't happen overnight," Sam said. He finally lifted his hand away from his face when a cloud blessedly covered the sun, allowing him to see. He smiled gently at Scarlett. "It's something that has to be worked at. And I want to be by your side as you do that."

"I...what?" Scarlett uttered, not entirely sure if Sam meant what she thought he meant.

"Scarlett, marry me. I've never cared about your family name or inheritance or anything else – I only care about you."

She frowned despite herself, resisting the urge to sigh in exasperation. "Sam, you *are* aware that I turned down Charlie and Mr Schmidt and Andreas three days ago, right? And I care deeply for all three of them – as I do you. So why do you think I would say yes to you?"

"Because, Miss Scarlett," Sam began, reaching out his hands to take one of hers. His fingers were large and rough and calloused; the hands of a hard-working, honest, down-to-earth young man who was currently wearing his heart on his sleeve. "Because, for me, there's only you. I don't want to marry you because you're the prettiest girl in town, or because my parents love you, or because I've known you the longest, or because I've been giving you flowers for years or I'm the perfect match to the Duke name. No, I...I just love *you,* Scarlett."

Scarlett stared at him, speechless. What was she supposed to say, anyway? That she didn't love Sam that way? That she had never viewed him as a 'man' before – because she'd never seriously viewed *anyone* like that before?

Except for Mr Wolfe, a small voice inside her head whispered, unbidden. *You've spent many a night thinking of him whether you want to admit it or not.*

"No, Sam," Scarlett eventually said in a small, small voice. His face fell immediately, hands slumping back to his side as his eyes filled with hurt and disappointment. "Sam, I – I'm not in love with you. I'm not in love with *anyone.* And I don't want to accept a proposal from a man I don't love. You must understand that."

Sam looked like he desperately wanted to argue. But he couldn't, for Scarlett was right. There must have always been a part of him that knew Scarlett did not feel for him the way he felt for her.

She touched his hand with gentle fingers for a moment, mouthed the word *sorry* and quickly hurried off, unsure what else to do in such a situation. She couldn't be angry at Sam's proposal; he had seriously thought about what to say and didn't force the conversation onto her. He had respected her. But that didn't make it any easier to respond to. If anything it made it even worse.

"How am I going to face him back at Nana's?" she said aloud as she escaped into a nearby side street, feeling mortified and terrible.

"Maybe you could feed him one of your grandmother's potions for a broken heart," an annoyingly familiar voice said from her right. "Telling him you don't love him and running off – what a cruel woman you are, Red."

She didn't have to turn her head to see who it belonged to.

CHAPTER TEN

Adrian

"I have to hand it to the Birch boy – he really tried hard with that proposal. Shame you turned him down flat."

"Go away, Mr Wolfe."

"Have I not earned being called by my first name yet, Red?" Adrian complained childishly. "I mean, we've already kissed and everything. I'd wager the only man who's gotten as close as that to you before is Mr Richard Duke himself."

"*You* kissed *me*," Scarlett bit back in a tone that very much suggested Adrian had done something far more disgusting to her. "And what are you doing eavesdropping anyway? Don't you have better things to do?"

"What, like listen to the same gaggle of young ladies unload all of their romantic woes on me? 'Mr Wolfe, how can I get him to notice me?' 'Mr Wolfe, do you have anything that would make me just a little curvier?' 'Mr Wolfe, Mr Wolfe, don't you have anything that will make him want to rip my –"

"I think I get it, *Mr Wolfe*."

Adrian chuckled; clearly Scarlett hadn't taken him abandoning her in the woods after being kissed very well. Her cheeks were flushed in irritation; brows knitted together. But Adrian didn't pay attention to her expression for very much longer when he had the rest of her to take in. For Scarlett had foregone her cloak, allowing him a rare view of her figure in a very flattering green dress. She didn't even have boots on today. Adrian wondered if she had put this much effort into her appearance for him; it was a thought he revelled in.

He sidled closer to Scarlett, appreciating the view down her dress he was granted by virtue of being taller than her. She glanced up at him and scowled.

"Get away from me, Mr Wolfe."

"Did you dress up just to turn the poor boy down?"

he teased, brushing a gloved hand against Scarlett's bare arm in the process. "Or was there somebody else whose attention you were hoping to attract? Because a certain somebody very much appreciates the absence of your cloak."

"I didn't even think you'd still *be* in Rowan, so how could I have dressed to attract your attention?" Scarlett said, rolling her eyes, though a subtle biting of her lower lip gave her away.

Adrian moved in even closer, resting an arm against the stone wall above Scarlett's head in order to box her in. "But you were hoping I hadn't left yet."

"If only so I could punch you in the face for accosting me in the woods yesterday."

"Is that what that was?" he murmured, dancing his fingers up Scarlett's arm whilst he watched her nervously react to his touch. "I seem to recall the young woman who was accosted wanting me to continue with said accosting."

Scarlett hesitated. Then, curiosity clearly getting the better of her, asked, "So why didn't you? Why did you leave when you did?"

"So that you'd spend all night thinking about me," he replied smoothly, which had genuinely been his intention. "Did you?"

"You're despicable."

"And yet you didn't answer the question."

"I don't owe you an answer. I don't owe you *anything.*"

Adrian lifted a hand to Scarlett's hair, so perfectly wound around her head. He played with the loose strands and, when she brought her hand up to stop him, slid his fingers straight through the flawless braid until it uncoiled down her back.

"Why would you do that?!" Scarlett exclaimed in outrage, pushing Adrian away from her in order to pull the braid over her shoulder and secure the bottom of it.

"I like it like this," he said simply, picking up the braid and dropping it down her back to emphasise his point. "It's easier to mess up. It was too perfect before."

Scarlett glared at him for a moment. But then her expression grew uncertain, as if she'd taken Adrian's words at more than simply face-value...which had been his intention.

"You're just looking for someone to amuse you whilst you're in Rowan. I'd be a fool to fall for your tricks only for you to disappear the second you got what you wanted."

And with that she turned and walked away, leaving Adrian momentarily stunned. He had never expected Scarlett to get caught up in a whirlwind romance the way the girls who swarmed his stall were desperate to, but even so – her response sounded like it came from a woman who was already weary of the world around her.

It caused him to wonder why Scarlett had refused no fewer than four proposals in as many days. None of her suitors were hideous to look at; in reality they were all handsome in their own way. If Adrian was being honest the blacksmith, Jakob, threatened him the most. He seemed the most forthright and least traditional of the men who had proposed to Scarlett...and the one most likely to try and bed her before marrying her.

"Scarlett, wait –" Adrian called out before he could stop himself, stepping away from the alleyway in order to follow after her, but he paused when he saw that Samuel Birch was walking straight up to her. He glanced at Adrian for a second as if he was deeply suspicious of the two of them having appeared from the same side street, then reached out for Scarlett's hand. Adrian forced himself to hang back to listen to what Sam had to say to Scarlett.

"Miss Scarlett, I'm sorry for pushing all of that on you," Sam hurriedly told her before she could protest. "It wasn't fair of me. I knew you weren't in love with me but I thought it didn't hurt to ask, anyway. I was wrong."

Scarlett sighed, then closed her hand around Sam's and squeezed slightly. Adrian bristled at the action. "Sam, you don't have to be sorry," she said, "but you can't expect me to suddenly accept a proposal out of the blue, either."

"I know, I know!" he replied enthusiastically, his eyes

100

bright with an intent that Adrian didn't like at all. "I realised I was doing everything backwards, because I was so worried about someone asking you to marry them first. And I *shouldn't* have been worried, because I knew there was nobody you held that kind of affection for. And yet still I panicked, because I..."

He shook his head as he laughed softly. "I'm an idiot, Miss Scarlett, and I make mistakes. But I learn from them. So let me learn from this one."

That seemed to pique Scarlett's interest. She cocked her head to one side. "And what do you mean by that, Sam?"

He moved in closer to her and took her other hand in his. Adrian had taken a step forwards in protest before he could stop himself, but then he felt a hand on his shoulder. Glancing behind him he saw Gerold and Frank, who were shaking their heads.

"Let the lad say his piece, you no-good Prince Charming."

Adrian rolled his eyes. "You're supporting *him*?"

"Over you? Any time."

"Thanks for the support."

And so Adrian stayed put with the other two merchants and continued to listen in on the conversation between Scarlett and Sam, whose blonde hair had turned to gold in the sun. It was almost too much to look at.

"If possible, Miss Scarlett," Sam explained, "could you maybe start looking at me as a man? You said before you'd never seen me that way. I'd very much like for that to change. And if, after you've gotten to know me like that, you still aren't interested in me, then I'll give up. I won't bother you on the matter, and we can remain as friends – if you want. I know I have no right to ask you to do this, but –"

"I think I can do that, Sam," Scarlett interrupted, smiling. Adrian almost thought he imagined it but he was certain she had glanced at him before replying to Sam's request. It was a glance that screamed *this is a man who won't run off.*

"Well if that's what you want, little miss, then that's what I'll be," Adrian muttered under his breath.

Without explaining himself to Gerold and Frank, and without so much as another look at the now-delighted Sam and lovely, smiling Scarlett, Adrian stalked over to the tavern and marched straight up to the barkeep, Mac.

"I'd like a room, please," he said, a determined grin on his face that Mac dutifully ignored as he wiped down the surface of the bar.

"For how long?"

"As long as necessary."

CHAPTER ELEVEN

Scarlett

"Here you go, Miss Scarlett."

"Thank you very much, Mr Macmillan."

"Call me Mac."

She smiled. "Thank you, Mac."

Scarlett rarely drank, having only ever indulged in warm, spiced wine in the depths of winter with her father and, later, her grandmother. Sometimes, when the weather was particularly lovely in the summer, her grandmother would serve her a lighter, paler wine diluted with freshly squeezed apples and berries.

Never had she touched beer, nor cider, nor spirits.

And yet here she was, in Gregor MacMillan's tavern, drinking her first tankard of ale by herself as if it wasn't the strangest thing anyone sitting at the bar had seen all day. For it was rare to have women in the tavern unaccompanied by male companions – let alone one young, lone woman such as Scarlett Duke. Many of the men in the tavern wanted to approach her.

Nobody had the courage to.

She had rejected four men since her eighteenth birthday, after all. *Four*! And all of various social standings. If money, family, status, looks or rogueish charm hadn't been enough for Miss Scarlett then the likelihood that any of the barflies had a chance with her was slim to none.

And so, even though many men wished to approach her or buy her a drink, Scarlett was left well alone. For that she was grateful.

She had broken away from Sam in the marketplace several hours prior and had spent much of her afternoon aimlessly wandering, for lack of anything better to do. Scarlett hadn't wanted to go back to her grandmother's, knowing that she'd have to tell the old woman about what Sam had said. She wasn't ready for that.

She wasn't sure she'd *ever* be ready for that.

For though Scarlett had agreed to Sam's second proposal – to start viewing him as a man instead of a friend – she had no idea how she was supposed to go about this. And she knew that her decision had been somewhat influenced by a desire to outwardly reject everything Adrian Wolfe stood for right in front of him. That part had been deeply satisfying, though when Scarlett had turned to see if the man was going to confront her he had gone.

She sighed. In all honesty Scarlett had absolutely no idea what she was doing. She had always thought life would somehow get easier when she reached adulthood – as if she'd innately know what to do in any given situation. But reaching an arbitrary age had, unsurprisingly, not granted her the experience and wisdom necessary to solve these situations.

Scarlett was on her own and she was hopelessly, dangerously clueless.

"Could I have another one, please, Mac?" she asked after a while. Though Scarlett couldn't profess to enjoying the taste of ale, the warm, buzzing feeling that was filling her from her head down to her toes was very enjoyable indeed. The barkeep nodded in acknowledgement as he poured her a new tankard and passed it over. She decided she liked Mac, who wasn't trying to impose on her solitude in the slightest.

Unlike Charlie Beck, who Scarlett caught out of the corner of her eye making a beeline for her the moment he entered the tavern.

"Hello, Miss Scarlett!" he exclaimed brightly as he sat by her side and then, to Mac, "I'll have what she's having." He turned on his stool to face Scarlett. "I've never seen you in here before."

"I figured it was worth seeing what all the fuss was about," she said politely, gesturing to her drink as she spoke.

He laughed. "All we do is waste our time and money and short-term memory in here. Best you stay out in the future."

Scarlett couldn't help but bristle at this. "I can do what I like, Charlie."

"Oh, I didn't mean it like that!" he quickly corrected, looking horrified. "I didn't mean to...sorry. I didn't mean to tell you what to do."

She raised an eyebrow before returning to her drink without another word.

Charlie shifted in his seat somewhat uncomfortably. "I heard Sam proposed to you today."

"What of it?"

"You didn't flat-out turn him down."

Scarlett sighed heavily, resisting the urge to run a hand across her face. "And I didn't say yes, either. Charlie, I'm not ready to marry anyone. But I...do know it wouldn't be you. I don't say that to be rude. I just don't see you that way."

Charlie seemed a little put out. "You told Sam you'd try to see him as a man, though..."

"Sam is – different. I think. I don't know."

"If you don't know then how could you know about *me*?"

Just as Scarlett was beginning to feel like she might lose her temper at Charlie's incessant protests Mac came over and handed the young man his drink.

"Miss Scarlett," he said, "I don't suppose I could ask you to take a few things up to one of the guest rooms on the first floor? It's too busy for me to leave the bar and my wife has stepped out to the butcher's."

The slight smile on Mac's lips told Scarlett that this was a lie. But he was providing her with a much-needed escape from Charlie that she wasn't in her right mind going to turn down.

She returned the smile with a broad one of her own, getting off her stool and walking around the bar to retrieve a tray of food and drink from the man. "Of course, Mac. Which room is it?"

"One-oh-three. It's at the end of the hallway once you climb the stairs. Thanks again."

Scarlett didn't bother to look back at Charlie or apologise for leaving the conversation so abruptly before she began her ascent. It was dreadfully rude of her, she knew, but then again – Charlie interrupting her obvious desire for solitude had been rude in the first place.

She reached the room in question frustratingly quickly. Knocking on the door once before swinging it open, she announced, "I'm just bringing up your meal from the – oh my *God*!"

For there, on the bed, lay a dishevelled Adrian Wolfe, his boots kicked to the floor, shirt undone and leggings unlaced. His hands were hidden somewhere beneath the waistband of the woollen drawers peeking out from beneath his leggings.

Scarlett turned around on the spot abruptly. She'd read enough books in her father's study – the ones she wasn't supposed to go near – to know what exactly Adrian had been doing.

Adrian stumbled off the bed until he reached Scarlett, pulling her back into the room as he simultaneously kicked the door closed.

"Seems like you caught me in a compromising position," he chuckled good-naturedly as he took the tray out of Scarlett's numb hands and placed it on a nearby dressing table. "Although, I have to wonder what kind of education you received to have known what I was about to do."

Scarlett was too mortified to look at him. "How do you even know that I knew what you were doing?"

"Your reaction speaks volumes, Red."

She took a step towards the door. "Well, you have your meal so I'll be –"

"Oh, I don't think you're going anywhere."

Scarlett frowned. "Who are you to tell me what to do?"

Adrian laughed, sliding a long-fingered hand up Scarlett's arm until he reached her shoulder. It sent her heart racing, especially when she realised he had no gloves on. It was the first time he'd ever touched her without them.

"I'm not telling you what to do; I'm merely stating what's invariably going to happen. I don't think you really *want* to go anywhere."

"And what makes you say that?" Scarlett asked uncertainly, achingly aware of every nerve Adrian's touch was setting on fire as his amber eyes scanned up and down her entire body.

"Why in the world would you willingly play the serving girl if not to get away from whatever – or whoever – is downstairs?" Adrian murmured. His fingers trailed up from Scarlett's shoulder along her collarbone, tilting her head to one side to follow the artery in her neck. Scarlett's whole body had gone numb; she couldn't move.

She didn't *want* to move.

"And what were you doing in Mac's tavern, anyway?" he continued, dropping his hand from Scarlett's neck to stalk around her slowly. She turned as he did, not daring to take her eyes off the man even for a second.

There was something different about Adrian that Scarlett couldn't quite place. Perhaps it was seeing him in a state of disorder, when usually he was immaculately dressed. Perhaps it was because he was a little drunk, if the empty tankards by his bedside were anything to go by. Perhaps it was the setting sun flashing through the window, turning his eyes molten as he devoured Scarlett with them.

"I'm a grown woman," Scarlet finally replied after far too long. "I can do what I like."

"Are you drunk?"

"Nobody gets drunk from one tankard of ale."

Adrian threw back his head and genuinely roared with laughter. "How naive you are, little miss. I know plenty folk who can't handle their alcohol. The question is – can you?"

Scarlett's cheeks flushed despite herself. "Do I seem like I can't, Mr Wolfe?"

"Adrian. Call me Adrian."

"It wouldn't be proper for me to call you so informally."

"And I'm telling you I want you to. Can't you abide

my request, Scarlett?"

Adrian had stopped circling now. He stood in front of Scarlett, reached out for her hand and edged backwards towards the bed. Just a little.

And then a little more.

Scarlett's eyes darted to the door and back again. "If I told you to let me go, would you?"

"If you meant it."

"...and what happens if I stay?"

A flicker of surprise crossed Adrian's expression, as if he hadn't entirely expected Scarlett to give in. With gentle, delicate fingers he began to unlace the bodice of Scarlett's dress. Slowly. Deliberately. Scarlett could only watch his face watching her as he did so.

"And what of your woodcutter, Red?" Adrian murmured as he finished with the laces. He slid the straps of the dress off Scarlett's shoulders; the bodice fell down to her waist, leaving her top half covered only by her low-cut, white blouse. "What would Samuel Birch say if he knew you were here?"

Scarlett narrowed her eyes for a moment. "Why would you ask me that now?"

"Because he asked you to see him as a man. But I don't think you'll be able to do that when you're allowing another man to undress you."

"Are you trying to shame me?" She held up her hands against Adrian's chest as if to push him; he held onto them instead.

One by one he kissed Scarlett's fingers. His breath tickled across her knuckles. She inhaled deeply, wondering if she really *couldn't* handle her alcohol and that this was all one huge mistake.

"Absolutely not," Adrian murmured. Quite suddenly, he let go of Scarlett's hands in order to deftly pick her up and drop her onto the bed, climbing on top of her before she had an opportunity to protest. He grinned. "I'm merely relishing in the knowledge that you turned Sam down – and everyone else, too – and yet here you are, with me. It's very satisfying. I didn't want them to touch you."

Scarlett's eyes went wide at the comment. "How long have you...wanted to touch me, Mr Wolfe?"

"Adrian."

He pawed at Scarlett's blouse without quite removing it, then allowed one hand to wander down to roam underneath her skirt. His fingers danced against her skin as they travelled along the length of her thigh. Scarlett thought that her heart would surely burst at the rate it was throbbing in her chest.

She locked eyes with him.

"Adrian," she whispered, "how long have you wanted to touch me?"

112

"Too long."

And then his mouth was on hers, hot and wet and hungry for Scarlett even as she gave into the same urges for him. Her hands found their way into his hair, insistently pulling Adrian closer, closer, closer.

Scarlett had never so desperately wished to be naked before. Her dress was a nuisance; her blouse in the way. But Adrian easily pulled the white fabric down as he trailed kisses from Scarlett's lips down to her breasts, gently biting and sucking on her nipples when he reached them.

She gasped at the sensation. It wasn't a feeling she was familiar with, but she found one of her legs curling around Adrian's back and pushing him against her in response. She felt a very telling hardness rub against her, below her stomach.

Adrian's breathing quickened. He pinned Scarlett down, lips back on hers as his tongue found its way into her mouth, stealing her breath away.

But just when Scarlett thought he was going to rip away the rest of her clothes – just when she was about to succumb to the unbearable urge to do the same to him – Adrian stopped.

He stopped.

It was as if every muscle in his body had grown tense and taut; his grip tightened painfully around Scarlett's wrists. When she opened her eyes there was a vein throbbing in Adrian's temple. His strange eyes had gone glassy, only serving to further make him look like he wasn't quite human.

"...out," he muttered through gritted teeth.

Scarlett gulped uncertainly. "Adrian?"

But then he violently threw her from the bed, chest heaving as he pointed at the door. "Out. Get out. Just... please. Get out."

Scarlett took a step towards him, confused and concerned. "Adrian, what's –"

"*Get out!*"

And so Scarlett left, hurriedly pulling the bodice of her dress back up as she wrenched the door open and slammed it shut behind her. Her heart was hammering painfully, both from excitement and abject fear.

For there was no doubt that Adrian Wolfe had indeed looked terrifying as he screamed for her to leave, with his feral eyes and lips drawl back into a ferocious snarl. It left Scarlett shaking her head in disbelief as she choked back the threat of tears in her throat.

Just what on earth happened to Mr Wolfe? Scarlett thought as she laced herself back up, feeling somewhat humiliated as she rushed down the stairs and out of the tavern without so much as a glance at anyone inside.

Above her the sun had set, leaving only the fat, silver moon hanging in the sky. It was a few days past full, leaving it looking somewhat lopsided. It made her feel even more miserable; she shivered as the chilly night air bit at her arms where Adrian's fingers had been mere moments before.

"I should have brought my cloak," she said to the moon as she began the long journey back to her grandmother's house. "...I never should have left it behind."

CHAPTER TWELVE

Adrian

He shouldn't have changed into a wolf. He'd already had his three days. So how had it transpired that Adrian had to unceremoniously throw a half-undressed Scarlett Duke out of his room before locking the door and clawing at his throat – a tell-tale sign that he was about to transform?

Before he lost his human form Adrian struggled back to the window, unlatching the lock and throwing it wide open. He was only on the first floor; once darkness had fully settled across Rowan he could escape across nearby rooftops and into the forest without being noticed.

But, for now, Adrian had to strip himself of all clothing and lie on the floor of the room he'd rented... and remain silent through the slow agony of losing his human form.

He clenched his teeth together as his bones cracked and split and stuck themselves back together in a disconcertingly familiar framework. His skull wasn't far behind the entire process; he bit back a yowl as his jaw broke apart only to grow longer and stronger before reattaching itself. His nails grew sharper and then his teeth did, too, filling out his muzzle. The hairs on his arms, then his legs, then the rest of his body, grew courser, thicker and darker.

When finally it was over Adrian was panting in dreadful pain. He thought one day he'd get over it. That he'd get used to it.

After six years he was certain that day would never come.

Jumping up onto the bed to poke his head out of the window, Adrian saw that the streets of Rowan were already quiet. He wasted no time in jumping to the nearest rooftop, clambering clumsily over the tiles before leaping over to the next roof, and then the next. He repeated this until he reached the very edge of the town, deftly dropped down to the ground and sprinted towards the forest.

The air whittled past his ears as he slalomed between trees and leapt over fallen trunks, racing towards Heidi Duke's house as fast as his legs would carry him.

He was furious.

He was humiliated.

He had probably ruined everything with Scarlett.

No, *he* hadn't ruined everything. Her witch of a grandmother had, and Adrian wanted to know why.

When he reached the old woman's front door Adrian knew he had beaten Scarlett there, even if she had gone straight home after he'd thrown her out. Heidi was standing outside her front door, her lined face accentuated by the light from the swinging lantern hanging above her.

Adrian stopped a few feet away from her and sat down on his haunches, staring at Heidi with a snarl on his face until her face broke out in a grin.

"What did you expect when you decided to stay here for another night, Adrian Wolfe?"

Adrian could do nothing but let a low growl simmer in his throat in response.

The old woman laughed. "I won't have that kind of attitude from you. So long as you choose to stay here longer than usual, I'll turn you into a wolf every night. I can't have you sticking your nose in where it doesn't belong – and don't think I don't know that you are."

For that moment he was glad he was a wolf and not a man, for if he were a man Adrian would have flinched. He wondered if Heidi had worked out he was trying to seduce Scarlett.

But how would she know? he wondered. *I doubt Scarlett would have told her anything.*

But then Adrian considered Heidi's accusation. It needn't be about Scarlett. It was more likely to do with the fact that Adrian knew what she was capable of as a witch. After selling her hemlock, perhaps Heidi was wary that Adrian was going to try and work out what she needed it for. This wariness wasn't unwarranted, of course; he *did* keep an eye on what she was working on when he was prowling about as a wolf.

But *she* couldn't know that.

He let out a whine.

"Don't give me that, you foolish man," Heidi said scornfully. "This was your own fault. I won't have you in my town longer than needs be. You'll be a wolf every additional night that you stay, you hear me? So why don't you do us both a favour and leave. I'm sure the young ladies in other towns are missing you dearly."

As she spoke, the tell-tale sounds of footsteps on the road not far from Heidi's front door caused Adrian's ears to stand up to attention.

Scarlett.

Her grandmother's face darkened immediately. "Get away from my house, Adrian Wolfe. Don't you dare let my grand-daughter see you or it'll be the end of you, I swear."

Letting out another low whine, Adrian turned tail and darted back into the darkness of the forest just as he was told. He didn't even turn back to look at Scarlett from the safety of the trees.

He couldn't. He would do something he'd later regret if he did.

With his tail thoroughly between his legs even as he gnashed his teeth in frustration, he thought bitterly about how difficult it was going to be to convince Scarlett to forgive his behaviour. Heidi Duke might have destroyed his ploy against her without even *knowing* she had. Adrian couldn't stand it.

I can't leave Rowan, he thought with grim determination. *I need to see this through to the end.*

And if that meant spending another few nights stuck in the body of a wolf then so be it.

CHAPTER THIRTEEN

Scarlett

Scarlett found herself standing outside the large, ornamental gates that opened onto the front gardens of the Sommer estate without really knowing how she had gotten there in the first place.

Why am I here? she wondered dolefully as the doorman led her through the gates, towards the entrance to the manor house. *It's not as if my father asked me to be here. There's nothing in it for me to act so polite on behalf of my family.*

Yet Scarlett knew she wouldn't turn back. It was the right thing to do, and the basket in her arms was laden with winter fruits, cured meats, wine and ale for the Sommers. It would be a waste to turn back now.

And besides, Scarlett was willing to do just about anything to stop herself from thinking about Adrian Wolfe, even if it involved coming face-to-face with Andreas for the first time since he had proposed to her. For how was she supposed to process the way Adrian had so viciously thrown her out of his room when they had been mere seconds away from ripping each others' clothes off?

She shook her head, face flushing in shame as she was escorted through to a parlour room. Scarlett couldn't believe she had allowed herself to get so carried away. It was unbecoming and reckless of her. Unbidden, she thought of how her father had, in rebellion against his arranged marriage, sought out another woman's arms and left her pregnant. The woman had been lucky in that Richard Duke went on to raise the child for her, but if Scarlett had actually slept with Adrian and gotten pregnant...

I don't know what I would have done, she shuddered. In reality it was good for Scarlett that Adrian had kicked her out, though the look on his face as he had demanded she leave still haunted her. He'd looked more animal that human – feral and violent and out of control.

And in pain, Scarlett couldn't help but add on. She

was deathly curious about what had happened to the man to cause him to act in such a way; however, dwelling on such a matter was pointless.

She had to get over him...even if part of her didn't want to. She had wasted too much of her time on the man already.

Sitting nervously in the parlour room with her basket of goods sitting on her knee, Scarlett wondered about what she was actually going to say to the Sommer family. *'Hello, I'm happy your son has returned in good health but perhaps you should teach him some manners'* seems *a little inappropriate,* she mused. *Just a little.*

But then the door to the parlour swung open and Otto Sommer, the ageing, most prestigious doctor in all of Rowan and its surrounding towns and villages, appeared, closely followed by –

"Scarlett?"

"Papa!" Scarlett exclaimed before she could stop herself, offloading her basket onto the nearest table in order to jump into his ecstatic arms. For Richard Duke was delighted to see his daughter in such an unexpected place; he hugged her tightly to his chest and kissed the top of her head as delicately as if she were a newborn babe.

"I'll give the two of you some privacy," Otto smiled. "Miss Scarlett, I'm afraid Henrietta and Andreas are out riding at the moment. I do apologise."

Scarlett curtsied deeply for the man after her father let her go. "It's my fault for arriving unannounced, Dr Sommer," she said politely. "I hope all is well with you."

"Very well now that my son has returned," he replied, "though I heard tale that he, ah, was a little *pre-emptive* in asking for your hand, my dear."

Scarlett blushed. "Perhaps a little. I admit I was more than a touch surprised."

Otto looked pointedly at her father. "Perhaps Andreas' proposal is something to discuss with your father. Heaven knows the boy has been badgering him for a meeting non-stop since his return!" He laughed good-naturedly before vacating the parlour room, leaving Scarlett and her father alone.

The pair embraced once more, Scarlett nuzzling her face against her father's chest whilst he stroked her hair. "I never expected to see you here, Red," he murmured.

"It was the proper thing to do, now that Andreas has returned. I thought..."

Her father broke the embrace to hold Scarlett at arm's length to take a proper look at her, as if calculating how much she had grown. "You thought what, my love?"

She sighed. "I thought it was the kind of thing you would want me to do. I know I'm not *really* a Duke or – or whatever – but –"

"Scarlett you will *always* be a Duke, no matter what,"

he replied, gesturing for Scarlett to take a seat on the expensively embroidered sofa behind them. He followed suit once she was seated, then clasped both of her hands in his own. "I know things are...complicated. That's all my fault. But I'm working hard to rectify that. Oh, Scarlett, the boys miss you so."

She felt her eyes begin to sting with the threat of tears. "I miss them, too. They must be getting so big! And I miss mo – Frances, too, though I don't imagine she would appreciate hearing that."

Her father sighed heavily. "She *would* appreciate that, though she's too proud to say as much out loud. Despite everything that's happened, my love, I'm quite certain she sees you as her daughter, whether that's obvious or not. And she misses you, though she won't admit it."

Scarlett somehow found this hard to believe, and though she didn't say anything about it her father could read it plain as day on her face.

He laughed. "Of course I understand why you wouldn't believe me. I think you just need to give her a little more time, if you could find it in you to do that."

"It's not like I have many other choices, do I?" she muttered, which only made her father laugh all the harder.

"You seem to have *many* choices, going by the number of proposals I've heard about over the last few

125

days. How many is it now – three?"

"Four," she corrected, grimacing slightly. "Samuel Birch asked me, um, yesterday."

Her father nodded. "I should have seen that one coming a mile off. My mother has told me about the boy's affection for you on numerous occasions."

Scarlett was surprised by this. Of course her father and grandmother talked, but it was a bizarre feeling to think that the two of them would talk about Scarlett when she wasn't there.

"If I'm being sincerely honest though, Red," her father continued speculatively, "then I'll admit that I really would love to see you married to Otto's boy. He's made it clear he cares not for your inheritance, nor for any children you would bear having any claim, either. They're a wealthy enough family in their own right. And Andreas is fond of you and easy on your eye, I'm sure. I don't think you could ask for much more out of a prospective marriage."

Scarlett was silent for a moment, staring at their entwined fingers as she thought about how to reply. She had always figured her father had wanted her to marry Andreas, though she hadn't known about their potential betrothal.

"Was it because of Frances that you never accepted Dr Sommer's offer to betroth me to Andreas, Papa?" she asked quietly. "Was it because it was a threat to Rudy and Elias?"

"Scarlett –"

"It's fine if it was. I understand. I just want to know."

She glanced up and locked eyes with her father; the truth was clear on his lined face. Scarlett saw that grey had coloured his luxurious, dark hair around the edges and peppered his closely cropped beard. For the first time in her life she saw that he was getting *old*.

For half a second Adrian Wolfe passed through her head, who didn't look like he was getting old at all yet had that perfect, white streak of hair breaking up the black. Scarlett realised she'd never had the opportunity to ask him if he dyed it.

Well I won't be looking for him to ask now, she thought sullenly. *He can go to hell.*

"Scarlett...?"

"Ah, sorry, Papa," she said hurriedly. "I'm afraid I've grown tired, and I have a long walk back to Nana's. I guess I'll have to come back when Andreas is actually home."

Her father smiled sadly. "I am so proud of you, Red."

"Then will you tell me?"

"Tell you what?"

"About my mother. Not today," Scarlett added on

when she saw a flash of panic cross her father's face, "but some day. It would mean a lot to me to learn about her... even if you don't know much."

He squeezed her hands. "Okay. One day. Let's repair our family and discuss it then. How does that sound?"

It sounded like more than Scarlett could have dared to hope for. It was everything she wanted.

Screw Adrian Wolfe, and all the other proposals I've had. They are nothing compared to getting my family back.

She grinned – a wide, infectious, genuine smile that her father eagerly returned.

"Like something I can agree to."

CHAPTER FOURTEEN

Adrian

Adrian had spent five days looking for Scarlett Duke. Five days with not a single sign of her dark hair or red cloak or wicker basket. He was beginning to wonder if he should simply visit her grandmother's house when, finally, Adrian spied her in Beck's bakery.

"Can you watch my stall for ten minutes, Frank?" he asked the man who was half dozing in a chair by his own stall. Not waiting for an answer, Adrian stalked purposefully over to the bakery and the promise of finally making up with the woman behind the window.

What he hadn't expected was getting waylaid by Samuel Birch.

"Leave her alone, Mr Wolfe."

Adrian blinked in surprise. Keeping his voice jovial and carefree he asked, "On whose authority should I leave her alone, Birch?"

But Sam was in no mood to deal with Adrian's mockery. He glared at him. "I know you're up to no good."

"And how would you know that?"

"You were eavesdropping when we were talking about Scarlett in Mac's tavern after her birthday. Everyone's seen you talking to her far more often since then. She seemed really bothered about something after you came by Old Lady Duke's house; she's not been herself since. And you cornered her in that alleyway a few days ago after I proposed to her. Whenever something's wrong with her you always seem to be involved."

Adrian quirked an eyebrow in amusement. "Is that all?"

Sam seemed angry beyond belief at Adrian's attitude. "Is that – is that *all*? Is everything a joke to you, Mr Wolfe?"

"Usually," he replied mildly. He ran a hand through his hair as he made to exit the conversation. "I don't see why me *talking* to a woman of age is so problematic, though. And it's not like Miss Scarlett and I are strangers."

He grinned wickedly as he said this, knowing exactly that it would have the intended effect of further infuriating Sam.

The other man grabbed onto the front of Adrian's shirt as he tried to walk away. "What have you done to Miss Scarlett?!"

Adrian held up his hands in mock surrender. "I didn't do anything as bad as you're implying, Birch. Or bad at all, to be honest. I saved her life."

Sam paused for a few moments, confused beyond belief at the comment. He narrowed his eyes. "You saved her...? When?"

"On her sixteenth birthday. I could have let the wolves have her. I didn't."

"You actually considered letting her die before saving her?"

"Of course not," Adrian lied smoothly. "I was merely pointing out I *could* have."

"You're despicable."

"Probably."

Sam seemed to consider saying something more but ultimately decided against it. He let Adrian go, glowering

131

at him one final time before saying, "Just leave her the hell alone."

As he began walking away, Adrian decided to bait the man for the sheer sake of it. "Well, we *did* kiss, actually," he remarked nonchalantly, as if what he was saying was nothing of importance. "More than once. Repeatedly, even. And –"

The rest of the sentence was lost to the sound of Sam's fist connecting with Adrian's face.

"You son of a – *leave her alone!*"

"Sam! Oh my God, Sam, what have you – Mr Wolfe?"

Adrian wiped at his nose, which was beginning to bleed in earnest. He winced at the pain spreading across his right cheekbone. *The bastard,* he thought. *That's going to bruise.*

But he smiled for Scarlett despite the pain. "Hello, Red. I've been looking for you. I'm sure you were aware."

Scarlett was frozen to the spot as her eyes darted from a furious, ruddy-faced Sam to a bleeding Adrian Wolfe. "What happened here?" she muttered, aware that the three of them were beginning to draw a crowd.

"Your boyfriend was merely telling me to stay away," Adrian said simply. "I retorted. He punched me. I deserved it."

"You admit that you deserved it?"

He laughed. "Naturally. It doesn't mean I'm sorry about what I said." Then his face grew a little more serious as he took half a step towards Scarlett. "Let me explain about what happened the other day. Please. I'm sorry."

"You're sorry for *what*?" Sam bit out, immediately suspicious.

Scarlett glanced at Sam one final time, then marched over to Adrian and ushered him away with her. Adrian couldn't quite believe it. Neither could Sam, who was shocked to speechlessness whilst he watched the pair of them walk away.

"I must admit I never expected you to speak to me again, Red," he said cheerily as they left Rowan behind, venturing towards the forest.

Scarlett scowled. "It's not what you think. I'm just... tying up loose ends. I'd keep wondering about what happened in Mac's tavern if I never asked you about it. But that's it. I have more important matters to concern myself with than you, Mr Wolfe."

"Are we really back to 'Mr Wolfe', Red?" Adrian sighed dramatically as they reached a small brook that ran along the fringe of the woods. Scarlett motioned for him to sit down on a fallen tree; he dutifully complied.

"It was a mistake to ever get on first-name terms with you," she murmured as she pulled a cloth out of a

133

hidden pocket in her dress. She wet it in the brook then went to work cleaning up Adrian's face, though his nose was still bleeding.

"It wasn't a mistake," he protested, voice nasally as Scarlett held the cloth over his nostrils. "What happened before – really, I'm sorry. It was abysmal timing."

Scarlett frowned, her lovely eyes shadowed by her brows as she inspected the tender flesh of Adrian's cheek. "What do you mean, 'abysmal timing'? What happened to you?"

"I have a...condition. A chronic condition."

"What kind of condition?"

"A painful one."

Scarlett looked at him pointedly. "You'll have to give me more than that."

"I don't – ah, that smarts –I don't know exactly what it is. Sometimes I'm hit by convulsions. Like a seizure. It's not pleasant. And it's painful. I didn't want you to see me like that...it's humiliating."

The best lies were those rooted in truth, Adrian knew, and nothing was truer than that last sentence.

Scarlett seemed taken aback by his explanation. "You haven't – you never told me about them before."

"Why would I? Nobody knows. If I can help it I make sure no-one is around to see me when I feel the convulsions begin. It's not exactly something I would share."

"You could have told *me...*" Scarlett muttered.

Adrian felt a glimmer of amusement at the expression on her face. She seemed put out by the fact he hadn't told her. He set about using this to his advantage, raising his hand to cover the one Scarlett was using to clean his face. He squeezed it slightly, never taking his eyes off of hers.

"I know. And I should have. I could have done with the help, actually; I could barely eat afterwards." He chuckled darkly. "I'm just not all that great on the honesty front."

"I surmised as much."

"Ah, but what about you, Miss Scarlett?" Adrian pondered as he stood up, bringing Scarlett along with him by her hand.

She stumbled slightly in surprise as he took them away from the road and through the sun-lit, frostbitten trees. "Where are we going, Mr Wolfe?" she asked. "And what do you mean 'what about me'?"

"We're just going for a walk," he replied, which was the truth. He simply wanted to make sure Sam or anybody else using the road through the forest didn't follow the pair of them and ruin the mood. He raised an eyebrow at Scarlett over his shoulder. "You'll accept going on a walk with me?"

135

"It seems like I don't have a choice."

"You always have a choice, Red."

Scarlett's cheeks flushed prettily at the comment. If Adrian wasn't treading on such thin ice trying to repair their relationship then he would have kissed her.

"And what I meant," he continued as he wound them expertly through the forest, "is that I don't know anything about you, in truth. You're very private. So tell me about yourself."

Scarlett stopped abruptly, causing Adrian to trip over the rotting carcass of a tree. She giggled despite herself. "How clumsy, Mr Wolfe."

"A moment I hope never to repeat," he muttered, feeling embarrassed despite himself. Falling over was *not* something Adrian Wolfe did...and certainly not when he was attempting to woo a woman.

"You say you know nothing about me," Scarlett mused, "but I know little and less about you."

"Your point being?"

Scarlett's lips curled up into the slightest of smiles. "Tell me about yourself first. Even the embarrassing things. Tell me it all."

Adrian couldn't help but laugh. "I'm a fairly boring person, really. I was hoping it would take a little longer for you to work that out."

"I think I'll decide that for myself. So...what makes you who you are, Adrian Wolfe? Will you tell me?"

He sighed for dramatic effect; Scarlett's smile grew wider.

"Fire away, Miss Scarlett."

CHAPTER FIFTEEN

Scarlett

"How long have you been working as a merchant, Mr Wolfe?"

"By myself? Since I turned twenty."

"Which was...?"

"Oh my, Red, are you so bold as to ask a man how old he is?"

"Only if the man is you...though I'd be inclined to believe you'd lie about it."

Adrian chuckled, letting go of Scarlett's hand in order to swing from a thick branch above their heads. He used the momentum to carry him over the stream they had been about to cross.

He flashed a grin as Scarlett rolled her eyes. "Show off," she murmured as she located a few rocks big enough to break the water's surface, nimbly jumping from one to the next until she reached Adrian's side.

"Nicely done, little miss. And I'm twenty-six. Twenty-seven in July."

"Huh."

"And what's that supposed to mean? I don't look older than that, do I? Is it the white in my hair?"

Scarlett's lips quirked as she took in Adrian's worried expression. "I knew you were a narcissistic man but I didn't realise you were *this* insecure, Mr Wolfe. And I assumed you dyed your hair, if I'm being honest. It's not artificial?"

He shook his head, fingering the white lock of his hair for a few seconds before pushing it back. "When my convulsions started the front of my hair just...lost its colour. I got quite depressed about it, actually."

"Strange that it stopped going white after just that one part, though," Scarlett said, eyeing up his hair curiously. "You sure you don't dye the *rest* of it to keep it black?"

"Now you're just being cruel. I don't need to do

anything to look as handsome as this. It's all natural."

Scarlett swatted his arm. "You are *so* full of yourself."

"Says the woman who has deliberately been making herself up to look as appealing as possible to me, even as she refuses to speak to me."

"Can't I look good for myself?" she muttered, crossing her arms protectively over her chest as she did so. Scarlett knew it made her look altogether like a petulant child; she didn't care.

Adrian undid the clasp of his cloak and swung the garment over an arm. "Of course you can, Red. Who do you think *I* make myself look good for?"

"You're infuriatingly full of yourself." Adrian shrugged at the comment, because it was true. Then Scarlett asked, "Aren't you cold?"

He shook his head. "I tend to run a little hot. I feel like I'm about to overheat merely looking at you in that fur hood."

"But it's so cold! I thought the weather was getting better but it's slipped right back into winter again. It's mid-April! What's going on?"

"Are we really going to talk about the weather, Red?"

Scarlett glanced up at the sky where a cloud had only just covered the sun, casting the pair of them in shadow. "The weather is interesting, though," she murmured, almost to herself. "The woods completely change

140

depending on the weather or the time of day. It's unsettling how comfortable I am here only to be terrified a few hours later. Do you not think so, too?"

Adrian seemed surprised by the comment. He scratched his eyebrow. "I guess I hadn't thought about it that way."

"How did you get that scar?"

Adrian paused before asking, "Which one?"

Scarlett raised her eyebrows. "You have more than one?"

"I have a few," he said, smiling mischievously. "If you ever feel inclined to undress me you'll see them all."

"You're...useless."

"It was a fair comment," Adrian laughed, "even if my *tone* was perhaps a little filthier than you wanted, Miss Scarlett."

She merely stared at him, arms still crossed over her chest in disapproval.

"Fine," he sighed, "fine. The one across my eyebrow is from a wolf. Same as the rest of them, actually."

"I – what? Wolves? What happened?"

"I was attacked," Adrian replied simply. "It was quite vicious. But I got away."

Scarlett took a few steps towards him, eyes glittering

with interest. "How did you get away? Did you kill the wolf?"

"No," Adrian replied softly. His expression seemed cagey to Scarlett, though she couldn't work out why. "I didn't kill the wolf. But I know the woods well. I got away."

Scarlett wasn't satisfied with his answer in the slightest. But there was something about the way Adrian was speaking to her that implied he wasn't going to elaborate. She decided to ask him about something else instead.

"Where are you from? Are your parents still alive?"

He shook his head. "Both dead. Most of the people in their village are dead, too. A plague," he explained, "though I survived. For a while afterwards I wished I hadn't. I didn't know what I was supposed to do on my own."

"Adrian, that's...awful," Scarlett said, at a loss for any other words. "I'm so sorry."

He waved a hand dismissively. "It's not like anyone could do anything about it. My mother was the healer for the village. As soon as she was hit by it we all knew the village was doomed. Sometimes I think my father only got sick because he had to watch her die."

"What did your father do for a living?"

"He was a con-man through and through," Adrian

chuckled darkly. He moved through the trees in silence for a while, Scarlett meekly following behind him. She had no idea where they were; she was completely disoriented.

"Nobody expected them to fall in love," he eventually continued, pausing in his tracks for Scarlett to catch up. He smiled somewhat sadly, though there was a fondness in Adrian's amber eyes that Scarlett had never seen there before. "But they did. My mother kept him on the straight and narrow as much as anyone could hope for...which wasn't much. I guess it's no surprise I ended up the way I am with such miss-matched parents."

"Is that why you sell legitimate medicine alongside all your ridiculous potions?"

"They're not actually ridiculous, you know," Adrian said, which surprised Scarlett. "They'd all do their jobs properly if I sold them at the right concentration. But can you imagine – a whole town of men and women ensorcelled on the whims of those wealthy enough to put something in their drink or cast a spell on them? Lord help you all if I actually sold products that worked properly."

Scarlett raised an eyebrow. "Why not simply...not sell them any of these things? Why not focus on being a healer?"

"Oh, come now, Scarlett, you can't be serious."

"What do you mean?"

143

Adrian faced her, taking her hand before bowing deeply and kissing her fingers. His eyes flashed wickedly when he saw her blush. "Do you know how much money I make from women looking at men the way you're looking at me now? And the other way around?"

Scarlett tried to pull her hand away in retaliation; Adrian pulled it closer towards him instead. "And even more than that," he murmured when their faces were inches from one another, "do you know how much people will pay for *revenge?* To get back at a lover who spurned them? To make a person who wronged them suffer?"

"...I imagine people pay a lot," Scarlett admitted quietly, thinking about the number of times she had fallen into despair over her own circumstances and wished for a way out. "Desperate people will do anything."

Adrian grinned, all sharp canines and even sharper amusement. "Exactly. And they're *all* desperate." He let go of Scarlett. "And they keep my business afloat. Being a healer alone isn't enough – not for a travelling merchant."

"So why don't you settle somewhere instead?"

"As if," he snorted, rolling his eyes at the apparently ridiculous idea. "Can you see me ever settling down?"

"...I guess not."

"Okay, Red; your turn."

144

He glanced at her when she said nothing. Scarlett sighed. She ran a hand through her long hair and shook it out from underneath the fur hood draped around her shoulders.

"What do you want to know?"

"Why were you really kicked out of the Duke residence? I don't see you as someone who did anything scandalous."

"You would be correct. It was my father who did something scandalous."

"Which would be?"

"He had me."

That froze Adrian in his tracks. "...your mother?"

"Frances Duke isn't my mother. I don't know who my mother is."

"So...your step-mother didn't want you standing in the way of her sons' inheritance? I take it that's the gist of it."

"Yes. But..."

"But?"

"I saw my father a few days ago. He thinks we might be able to fix things – as a family."

Adrian smiled. "And that's all you want, isn't it?"

Scarlett's eyes were wide as she nodded. "More than

145

anything else in the world."

"Oh, but...wait." Adrian scratched his head in confusion. "So when the blacksmith and the doctor and the baker all proposed to you, they didn't care that you weren't going to inherit your father's fortune nor his estate?"

"I told them and none of them rescinded their offers," Scarlett replied bashfully. "In truth I thought it would dissuade them. I thought wrong."

"I don't think you put enough stock in your individual worth, Scarlett Duke."

And then Adrian kissed her, but it wasn't rushed or forceful. It was soft, polite and chaste against her lips. It was a kiss Scarlett would never have thought he was capable of.

"We've reached your grandmother's house, Red," he murmured with a soft smile that genuinely reached his eyes. "Thank you for telling me about your family."

Scarlett hardly dared to breathe. Everything that she had decided merely days ago – that she was done with Adrian Wolfe, that he wasn't worth her thoughts and attention – had been thrown out of the window. The man in front of her was...different. He was someone Scarlett very much wanted to spend time with. Someone she wanted to –

"Thank you for telling me about yours," she echoed back. Her fingers twitched with the desire to reach out and touch Adrian's face.

She resisted.

"I better be getting back to my stall," Adrian finally said. "Frank will be furious with me leaving for so long. And he'll be dying to know why I got punched in the face, too."

Scarlett chuckled despite herself. "It's going to bruise."

"I know."

"Your handsome face will be spoiled."

"Good to know you think me handsome, little miss."

Adrian grinned at the scowl on Scarlett's face – and then he was gone.

Scarlett held a hand up to her lips, fingers tracing where Adrian's mouth had been on hers. Her heart wouldn't slow down, thumping ever more painfully against her ribcage as she watched him walk further and further away.

I'm in deep trouble, she thought.

CHAPTER SIXTEEN

Adrian

Adrian was conflicted – a feeling he never thought he'd associate with himself. But here he was, conflicted, confused and capricious as hell.

I like her, he thought as he paced back and forth through the forest. *I genuinely, hopelessly like her.*

There was nothing else to it; Adrian Wolfe was more than merely physically attracted to Scarlett Duke, which threw a wrench in his plans he'd never had the foresight to consider.

And yet I'm a wolf! Adrian paced back and forth in the woods, bushy tail swinging behind him in frustration. *We're practically at a new moon and I'm still a wolf because of her grandmother. And I'll remain tied to this curse for as long as the damn hag wishes.*

Adrian wanted out. He was desperate for it. Though he was genuinely fond of Scarlett, escaping his damnable curse had to be his priority...even if he hurt Scarlett in the process.

A gnawing hunger ate at his stomach, causing Adrian to regret not having eaten before transforming. He didn't feel much up for hunting through the woods, though he had no patience for feeling hungry, either. And so, knowing that a few, errant deer could often be found close to Heidi's house by virtue of the other wolves being scared of the place, Adrian began to lope through the dark underbrush of the forest in the direction of her house.

If he were a man he would have laughed bitterly at the fact that a tiny, unassuming house in the middle of the woods of Rowan would be home to *both* of his tormentors. The one he couldn't stand had her nails digging ever more sharply into his soul; the other seemed to be stroking ever more insistently and distractingly at his heart...and somewhere else, too.

For Adrian knew that part of the hunger he was feeling had nothing to do with food. That feeling was only growing stronger every moment he spent with

Scarlett, and getting worse every moment he spent *without* her.

It wasn't something Adrian was used to. Until recently if he felt an insatiable desire for a woman he'd simply...find one. It was easy to charm and seduce a woman into bed when he had entire towns full of them to choose from. But it was different now; if the woman wasn't Scarlett then Adrian didn't want her – even though he knew he was planning on discarding her in order to lift his curse.

He thought dolefully about how his situation would be so much better if he didn't actually hold Scarlett in any high regard. It made it even worse that she was painting her lips and braiding her hair and wearing low-cut dresses for the sole purpose of enticing Adrian, whilst at the same time (rightfully) keeping a wall up against him. It was infuriating. He wanted the woman and he wanted her *now.*

Well, not whilst I'm a wolf, Adrian thought as he reached his destination. *But if I don't get Scarlett into bed in the next day or so I might well go insane.*

The fact that he had to get her into bed during daylight hours made things even more difficult. People were far too proper during the day; it was much easier to entice and persuade and bewitch them under a murky, moonlit sky.

Adrian searched around the stone walls of Heidi Duke's house on soft, silent feet. The scents he picked up weren't promising – no deer had been close to her garden for hours. And yet he didn't want his search to have been in vain, so Adrian continued prowling around for another half an hour, nose swinging from the ground to the air in an attempt to pick up a promising scent.

All he could smell was Scarlett.

Don't go to her window, Adrian thought even as his wolf body ignored the command and stalked around to the back of the house, where Scarlett's bedroom was. Her window was ajar, which explained why Adrian could pick up the intoxicating smells of vanilla, saffron and sandalwood so strongly. There was a warm, soft light just barely shining through the glass, telling him that Scarlett was likely not yet asleep, which of course was even more reason for Adrian to retreat back into the shadows.

He didn't.

Padding over to the windowsill he stood up on his hind legs to place his front paws on the ledge in order to better see into Scarlett's room. The warm light Adrian had seen through the window was from her fireplace, where the roaring flames danced and crackled as if they were alive.

Adrian flinched despite himself; as a wolf he was instinctively, deathly afraid of fire. The feeling often seeped into his true form, causing him to shy away from fireplaces in taverns and inns even though he knew they posed him no harm. He had to wonder why Scarlett had her window slightly open when she had a fire going to keep the room warm in the first place.

The young woman in question wasn't actually *in* her room, sending a wave of disappointment over Adrian. But just as he wondered whether he should turn and leave she appeared, humming tunefully and wrapped in a robe as if she'd only just bathed.

He lowered himself from the ledge ever-so-slightly, reducing the risk of Scarlett spying him through the window. Adrian almost felt as though he was holding his breath when she disrobed, revealing that she was wearing nothing underneath. Thinking briefly of Sam Birch having witnessed a similar sight, Adrian happily agreed with what the man had said about Scarlett's body – it was perfect.

The warm glow from the fire cast her pale skin in amber light, revealing a fine mist of water still clinging to her from the bath. Scarlett's long, beautiful hair was tied back in messy disarray, but now that she had returned to the confines of her room she released it, sending it tumbling down her back. The action caused a fresh wave of her scent to roll over Adrian's nose; he found himself salivating and holding back a whine of longing as a result.

How can she be this unguarded when she knows Sam saw her through her window? Adrian thought, despite the fact he was thoroughly enjoying the view. But he didn't want anybody else to see Scarlett like this. To that end he wished he could cover up the glass and protect Scarlett's modesty on her behalf.

Scarlett rubbed at her shoulders as if working out a knot in her neck. Adrian watched her do so, transfixed by the way her breasts lifted when she raised her arms. She continued to hum some unknown tune as she turned to look in her mirror and inspect her face, giving Adrian full view of her body from behind. The shadows in the fire-lit room only served to accentuate each and every curve of her.

He dug his claws into the window-ledge.

If Adrian hadn't known any better he'd be convinced Scarlett knew she was being watched. He didn't see why, otherwise, she would masquerade around her room completely naked for so long and in such a sensual manner.

When finally she laid down on her bed Scarlett did so without putting on any clothes. She merely pulled back the sheets and snuggled beneath them, content in the warmth of the fire and the freshness of the low, icy breeze blowing through the gap in her window.

Adrian couldn't stand knowing that she was wearing nothing under the sheets. He thought of the morning, and the possibility of Sam Birch catching Scarlett, once more, completely naked and unaware. Sam had asked Scarlett to start viewing him as a man; perhaps he would use the opportunity to demonstrate just how *much* of a man he was.

Adrian let out a near-silent growl at the thought, the vibrations of the noise running all the way along his spine. But it was loud enough to alert Scarlett to his presence. For the second time in his wolf form Adrian froze in place, eyes locked on Scarlett's as she watched him with an expressionless face.

He wondered what she would do. His behaviour was clearly unnatural for a wolf – Adrian had no idea how Scarlett would explain it away. He highly doubted her mind would immediately come to the conclusion that the wolf outside her window was actually a man, regardless of the fact that that was indeed the case.

To Adrian's surprise Scarlett's lips curled into the slightest of smiles as she sat up in bed. The sheets fell around her hips, exposing her body from her neck down to her waist. Adrian could do nothing but stare. Scarlett was *letting* him look.

What is wrong *with this woman?!* he thought, simultaneously confused and excited beyond belief. Nobody in their right mind undressed for a wild, vicious animal.

Nobody except Scarlett Duke.

"What is it that you want, Mr Wolf?" Scarlett murmured, just loud enough for Adrian to hear. She slid all of her hair over one shoulder and began to play with it, teasing out errant knots and tangles with quick, nimble fingers as she kept her beautiful eyes on Adrian.

He whined.

He licked his lips.

He ran away.

For what could Adrian do as a wolf? He darted back into the woods, never more frustrated not to be a man than he was now. Even after rutting against a fallen tree trunk he couldn't get rid of his dissatisfaction.

He couldn't bear to play the long game anymore. No longer could he toy with Scarlett's affections – having her give in and making her want more only to pull back for her to yearn for him all the harder. He was done. Adrian's body couldn't take it.

Tomorrow he'd properly seduce Scarlett once and for all.

CHAPTER SEVENTEEN

Scarlett

"Mr Schmidt?"

Jakob took a few seconds to realise somebody was calling his name over the sounds of his hammer. But when he eventually looked up and saw Scarlett his work was quickly abandoned.

"To what do I owe the pleasure?" he grinned, wiping away the fine layer of black soot that had accumulated on his brow before ushering Scarlett inside his workshop.

Scarlett smiled demurely. "I think it's about time we

talked properly about your proposal, Mr Schmidt."

Outside the workshop the threat of rain hung ominously in the air. It was early morning – many of the streets of Rowan were still quiet – and Scarlett was keen to return to her grandmother's house before the clouds finally released the downpour they were carrying. But she was determined to tie up all the loose ends that were the proposals she'd been given so that, if and when Frances Duke was willing to welcome Scarlett back into the family, she brought no complications along with her.

And so here Scarlett was, in Jakob Schmidt's smithy, preparing to turn him down even as he realised that was exactly what she was doing.

"You turning me down flat, Miss Scarlett?" Jakob asked as Scarlett made her way around the workshop floor to where he stood.

She glanced at her feet when she reached him. "I... don't want to marry anyone right now."

Jakob chuckled. "So I might still have a chance?"

"Possibly. But – not likely."

"Ouch. That stings, Miss Scarlett. But this means you're turning down Andreas too, then?"

He didn't mention Charlie. He had never viewed the baker's boy as a threat.

Scarlett grimaced somewhat as she fiddled with the fastening of her red cloak. "I think my father would want me to marry him. But I barely know Andreas anymore. He's a fully-fledged adult now."

"But so are you."

"Which makes it all the more confusing. I don't really know who *I* am now. I'd like to take some time to find out, I think."

Jakob sighed magnanimously, then turned from Scarlett to rummage through a drawer for something. When he returned he was holding a perfect imitation of a snowdrop, cast in silver and so achingly beautiful Scarlett almost cried.

"This is for you, Scarlett. I *had* meant it as a wedding gift, but...you turning down everyone to take care of yourself first is just as good a reason for me to give you it."

He proffered it to Scarlett, who didn't move at first. She eyed Jakob curiously. "This...for me? Truly? No strings attached?"

He laughed. "Maybe once you're done working out who you are you can entertain the idea of me taking you out for dinner. But no pressure – I was wrong to have sprung my proposal onto you in the first place. I'm a grown man; I should have known better."

"You've always been a competitive man, Mr Schmidt," Scarlett said, smiling slightly as she finally took the snowdrop. "It's not surprising that you fought hard to out-do Andreas and Charlie."

He chuckled at the comment, then asked, "Pray tell, Miss Scarlett – who out of all your suitors would you have been most inclined to choose, if you were going to choose one of us at all?"

Scarlett's mind flashed immediately to Adrian Wolfe, though he wasn't one of the suitors to which Jakob was referring. Her face flushed at the question. "I must admit...probably you. Although I don't see a marriage with you lasting all that long. You seem a little, um, *too* passionate for me to handle."

What Scarlett meant was that Jakob was known to have an insatiable appetite for women, and he knew this. For a few seconds he didn't respond but then he roared with laughter. Eyes glittering, he put both his hands around Scarlett's and squeezed slightly.

"Ah, you really are a keeper. A sharp tongue and honest to a fault. Any man would be lucky to have your affections. So what about Samuel Birch?"

Scarlett blinked. "...what about Sam?"

"Come now, Scarlett. He follows you around like a lost puppy. You didn't even have the heart to properly reject him. Seems like he found the best way to try and win you over in the long-term."

She looked away uncomfortably. "I don't – that's not really what happened, Mr Schmidt. Regardless, when I say I'm not ready to marry anyone I mean it. With that in mind how I feel about Sam right now shouldn't really matter, should it?"

Jakob sighed as he let go of her hands. "You really have grown up. That was a more adult response than any I've heard from half the adults around here. I have no doubt you'll choose well if – and when – you do." He glanced outside when a gust of wind blew through the workshop. "I'd wager you should get back to your grandmother's before the weather gets worse, Miss Scarlett."

She nodded, carefully tucking the beautiful, silver snowdrop into the inside pocket of her cloak before pulling her fur-lined hood up and over her head. "Thank you for being so understanding, Mr Schmidt."

"Call me Jakob," he replied as Scarlett turned to leave.

She smiled. "Then have a good day, Jakob."

Jakob stared at her regretfully. "You really won't reconsider my proposal?"

"Good-bye, Jakob."

"You're a cruel one, Scarlett!"

The words followed Scarlett as she rushed back to her grandmother's as quickly as she could. It was something Adrian had said to her, too, and made her wonder just how cruel she actually was.

I never mean to be, she thought, wincing when a few icy drops of rain hit her face. Pulling her cloak around her a little tighter, Scarlett picked up her walking pace and powered through the unseasonably wintry weather until, with some relief, she spied her grandmother's house just as the rain truly began to fall.

"Nana, I'm back!" Scarlett called out after she struggled to close the heavy kitchen door against the wind. But nobody responded; the kitchen was dark and empty. No fire sat in the fireplace. Somewhat concerned, Scarlett moved through the house only to discover that her grandmother was nowhere to be seen. When she returned to the kitchen she realised there was a letter on the table. Frowning, Scarlett picked it up to see what it said.

It read: *Emergency supply run with Samuel to Burdich; your father kindly provided a horse and carriage. Won't be back before nightfall and may stay overnight so don't wait up. All my love, Nana.*

Scarlett was stunned. Her grandmother rarely travelled outside of Rowan and her beloved woods. Burdich was at least three hours away by horse and carriage – longer with the weather having taken such a bad turn.

What on earth was so important to buy that she had to travel in this rain? Scarlett worried. *She'll get sick.*

She felt a pang of frustration towards Sam, whom Scarlett should have been able to trust to dissuade her grandmother from going on such a journey.

161

"Men are useless..." she muttered as she shirked off her cloak, shivering at the chill in the air. Scarlett glanced at the empty fireplace in the kitchen, then, upon realising she was likely not to spend much time anywhere else but her bedroom for the rest of the day, took an armful of firewood and moved through to get the fireplace going in her own room, instead.

It took a long time for the air to finally warm up. Scarlett changed into a long, white, sleeveless nightgown that tied at her waist and huddled against the fire, feeling abruptly clueless about what to do until her grandmother's return.

Much of her time lately had been spent either thinking of, avoiding or interacting with Adrian Wolfe. She didn't much like acknowledging that fact especially because it was painfully true. And Scarlett was desperate to see him again – though she had to admit feeling somewhat apprehensive about what would happen when next they actually saw each other.

But she was excited, too. Her insides coiled up at the thought, a simultaneously pleasant and frustrating sensation that she couldn't get rid of. Determined to think about literally anything else Scarlett pondered the wolf that had been lurking outside her window the night before. It was the same wolf she had seen two weeks before, she was sure.

But as she remembered how brazen she had acted upon noticing its presence Scarlett's face only grew hotter.

"What's wrong with me these days!" she exclaimed, for nobody to hear but herself. "I must be going insane."

For she could find no explanation for her thoughts and behaviour other than madness. Scarlett wasn't acting like herself at all. She wondered if this was what it meant to be an adult.

As the wind and wild, torrential rain continued to roar outside her window, Scarlett huddled closer to the fire. Even if it was a sign of madness she still longed to see Adrian, especially because she was alone.

Such things don't happen just because one wishes for them, she thought.

Then she heard a banging noise coming from the kitchen.

A knock on the door.

CHAPTER EIGHTEEN

Adrian

The storm had well and truly hit Rowan by the time Adrian finally made his way towards Heidi Duke's house in the woods. Though it was only early afternoon the thick, purple clouds and sheets of rain cast the woods in an eerie kind of twilight, which set Adrian's teeth on edge when he thought about having to transform in a few hours.

Adrian wasn't sure what he planned to do; it wasn't as if he could seduce Scarlett whilst her grandmother was there. He'd wanted to run into her in Rowan, of course, but Scarlett had already been and gone from the market square by the time Adrian had changed back into a human, emerged from the forest and made himself look presentable enough to see her.

But he needed to see her.

He was desperate to see her.

And so Adrian came upon the house sodden and frozen to the core, which was largely his own fault for not wearing a cloak. "So much for running hot," he muttered through gritted teeth. He guessed even the endurance his wolf form granted him had its limits – and pouring, bitter rain was it. His white shirt was translucent against his skin, his black waistcoat and leggings sticking to him in an uncomfortably thick, slimy manner. His leather boots had long-since soaked through.

It was only when he reached the front door that Adrian realised there was no fire going or lights on in the kitchen, though the lantern above the porch was lit. He became abruptly aware of the fact that there might be nobody in. He didn't know how he was supposed to cope with that, so Adrian ignored the growing feeling of dread and disappointment creeping up his spine as he knocked upon the heavy door.

He rapped his knuckles politely against the grain at first, then banged more insistently when even he couldn't hear the sound his hand made over the thunderous wind.

"Tonight is going to be so much fun," Adrian

murmured humourlessly, thinking about how miserable being a wolf in such a storm would be. He only hated Heidi Duke all the more for her damnable, merciless curse because of it.

But all thoughts of the old woman were lost when the front door finally opened and Adrian came face-to-face with a very confused-looking, red-cheeked Scarlett.

Her eyes grew wide as she took in the sight of Adrian, shivering and dripping wet beneath the fluttering light from the lantern above him, which was swinging dangerously in the wind.

"Mr Wo – Adrian!" she exclaimed in disbelief. "What are you doing here? You're absolutely soaking! Have you taken leave of your senses altogether?"

He tried to smile in response; it came out as more of a grimace. "Quite possibly. Is your grandmother in? I wanted to raid her stores from the mountains."

Scarlett paused for a moment, eyebrow quirked at the explanation as if she wasn't sure whether to believe it or not. "She isn't here," she eventually said. "Nana and Sam took one of my father's carriages to travel through to Burdich for some essential supplies. They won't be back until after nightfall, she said."

Adrian flinched despite himself. Anything Heidi Duke would travel out of Rowan for in such horrendous weather couldn't be anything good. But when Scarlett looked at him in concern he shrugged off the flinch as a reaction to the howling wind.

"May I come in anyway?" he asked, gesturing around in the general direction of the storm. "It's not very pleasant out here."

Scarlett burst out laughing at the comment despite herself, then retreated from the doorway to let Adrian into the kitchen. It was only after she slammed the door shut behind him that she truly took in just how wretched the man looked.

"Why on earth were you travelling without a cloak on?" she demanded, hands on her hips as she scanned over his appearance with an affronted look on her face. "It's dangerously cold out there – you could have killed yourself!"

It made Adrian want to kiss her, to see her so concerned for his health. He tried to chuckle through chattering teeth as he shook dripping wet hair out of his eyes like a dog. "I run –"

"Don't you dare say you run hot, Mr Wolfe. You're freezing."

Scarlett's fingers trailed along Adrian's arm just long enough to feel how truly cold he was before flinching away from the sodden material.

He glanced around the kitchen. "It's not much warmer in here, to be fair. How are your cheeks so rosy, Miss Scarlett? And I see you're once more not dressed appropriately for entertaining strange men – or the cold."

Scarlett only blushed harder at the comment. Though her night gown was certainly longer than the previous one Adrian had seen her in, the thin straps had fallen from her shoulders, giving him an enticing look at the curves of her breasts and the promise of the rest of her nakedness beneath the thin fabric.

When she realised Adrian's attention had very much diverted from the cold to her body she gulped slightly, then turned for the corridor. "I have a fire going in my bedroom. Come through and take your clothes off to dry by it."

"Well that is quite possibly the most wonderful invitation I've ever received," Adrian remarked, his tone filthy as he began to unlace his shirt with fingers made clumsy from the cold.

Scarlett threw an expensively-woven towel at Adrian's face. "You can make jokes when your teeth stop chattering, you idiot."

Adrian was thoroughly enjoying this version of Scarlett; he could only assume it was how she looked after her brothers. And so he complied, wincing as he struggled out of his sodden clothes and boots full of ice water. When Scarlett finally turned to face him once more he was rubbing his hair dry with the towel whilst the rest of him was stark naked, revelling in the heat from the fire. She immediately looked away again.

"The towel was to cover your – you know."

Adrian could only laugh. "Are you embarrassed, little miss? You'd have seen a lot more back at Mac's tavern if I hadn't...had a fit."

She glanced at him for half a second before busying herself with picking up his discarded clothes, laying them over the metal grille that stood in front of the fire to protect the floor from getting scorched. Adrian followed suit and picked up his boots, resting them by the hearth before retreating from the flames as quickly as he could without raising any questions pertaining to his unreasonable fear of them.

"Your scars," Scarlett ended up saying, sparing another glance at Adrian's chest, and then another. "You weren't lying about them."

"Of course not," he replied, turning around to give Scarlett a full view of the ones on his back, too. Though most of his scars were now years old and well worn into his skin, there were a few from the turn of the year that were still shiny and new. "Do they make me less handsome?"

Scarlett snorted derisively. "You must know that they don't."

Adrian flung himself on top of Scarlett's bed before she could stop him, revelling in her scent even as she let out a noise of shock at his literal and figurative boldness.

"Don't lie on my bed when you have nothing on, Adrian!" she complained, rushing over as if to push him off before thinking better of it when she ended up staring far too long at his entire body stretching out in front of her.

He could only grin. "I'm tired from my long journey through the storm. I need to rest, do I not? How do you smell so good, Scarlett? What is it that you use?"

Scarlett froze to the spot, shocked to speechlessness by the dramatic change of subject. She faltered for a moment before replying, "It's an oil that my mother – that Frances – has always used. Her grandfather was from somewhere abroad. I loved the way she smelled, so my father started importing more of the oil just for me to use years ago."

Adrian sighed contentedly as he closed his eyes and nuzzled into the sheets of her bed. Usually it was only as a wolf that he could fully appreciate the smell of her, but literally surrounded by objects belonging to Scarlett he could finally experience it as a human. The vanilla was so fragrant he could almost taste it.

"So good..."

"Adrian...?" Scarlett murmured uncertainly, for it very much seemed as if the man truly was intending to rest as he said. "Are you really just going to sleep on my bed?"

Half-opening his eyes he peered at Scarlett, the hint of a smirk playing across his lips as he said, "Am I really *just* going to sleep on your bed? What are you hoping for, Miss Scarlett?"

Scarlett ran a hand through her hair – a gesture that was simultaneously nervous and annoyed – before making to turn from Adrian. But he flung an arm out and grabbed her far more quickly than Scarlett could ever have imagined a human was capable of moving and, before she knew it, Adrian had pulled her onto the bed and held her in place above him. Scarlett's eyes grew wide for a moment, then her eyelashes fluttered down as Adrian gently stroked the inside of her right wrist with his thumb.

"I'll be honest, Red," he purred, his eyes like fire in the warm glow of the room as he stared up at Scarlett's uncertain, excited face, "I have no intention of sleeping whatsoever. What about you?"

Her eyes grew heavy-lidded. She took a deep, shuddering breath. Then Scarlett reached down until she was almost close enough to touch Adrian's lips with her own. Tendrils of her dark, lustrous hair tickled the skin of his cheekbones.

"I don't feel much like sleeping, either."

Adrian's mouth was on hers before Scarlett even finished the sentence.

CHAPTER NINETEEN

Scarlett

Scarlett's body was tingling with fire and passion and heat, heat, heat. Her insubstantial nightgown was all but torn from her body before she had time to catch her breath from the first of many blisteringly demanding kisses Adrian landed on her lips. It was as if he would die if he let go of her for even a second.

It only made her want him all the more.

Adrian's hair was still wet from the storm which continued to batter on outside the window, turning the afternoon into twilight as Scarlett ran her fingers through the one, solitary streak of white in amongst the black. When she pulled on his hair, urging Adrian to deepen their kiss, his tongue found his way into Scarlett's mouth even as his hands crawled all over her body pulling her towards *him.*

"You have no idea how long you tortured me, Scarlett," he growled in a fleeting moment between kisses, his words becoming a groan when Scarlett dared to brush a hand between his legs. Adrian squeezed his thighs around it, trapping her delicate fingers there. She gasped slightly when he toppled her beneath him on the bed.

"How was I to know?" Scarlett asked, breathless. Some animal instinct that had always known what to do from the moment she met Adrian caused her to dig her nails into his thigh and, when he let go of her hand in surprise, she grabbed hold of the length of his erection.

Adrian ran his lips down her neck, biting down against the artery there ever so slightly when Scarlett began stroking him. His fingers nimbly fondled her breasts before creeping down across her navel; her mouth formed a wordless *oh* when they travelled down even further.

"Surely you noticed me watching you over the last two years," Adrian whispered into Scarlett's ear. "For how could I not, after you ran into my arms the night you fled into the woods?"

Scarlett's breathing hitched as Adrian's fingers moved faster; more insistently. Her own hand matched his pacing until he reached for it and pulled her wrist up and over her head.

His eyes glowed dangerously in the firelight. "You're too good at that to be an innocent virgin, little miss. Do you know that?"

Scarlett laced her legs through Adrian's as she let a self-satisfied smirk cross her lips. "Maybe I'm just naturally talented."

"A talent I'd rather nobody else was aware of," he chuckled, kissing each of her breasts in turn before returning to her lips. It wasn't long before Scarlett's breathing became so fast that she was worried she would hyperventilate.

"Adrian –" she began, but he merely grinned wickedly before sliding his fingers inside of her. The rest of Scarlett's sentence was lost to pure shock and pleasure; a few, scant seconds later and she was moaning against Adrian's lips, struggling against his grip on her other hand to let her go. "Adrian," she cried out again, "let me touch you, let me –"

So Adrian let her go just as Scarlett climaxed, her fingers satisfyingly clinging into his back as her body was overwrought by wave after wave of tingling, ecstatic satisfaction. Scarlett felt like she could barely breathe because of it.

Adrian ran a hand through her hair, sliding his entire body against Scarlett until she bit back a cry.

"I'm – it's so sensitive. Adrian, be careful –"

"Careful is for later," he replied, eyes glittering. "It's my turn now."

And then the full length of him was inside Scarlett, and this time there was no biting back the noise that came from her throat. Her fingernails dug into his back, only digging deeper when Adrian began to grind against her.

"Oh God, oh –"

Adrian smothered her words with his mouth. "You're okay, Red," he murmured, the words tickling her lips as he spoke them. "Just trust me."

Scarlett didn't know what else she could do *but* trust Adrian Wolfe, given the situation. Though she gladly did so; now that the initial shock of pain was over her body was growing accustomed to the feeling of the man inside of her. A few more seconds passed and Scarlett began to crave more – for Adrian to hit harder, and faster, and deeper.

She ran her hands through his hair, pulling him closer against her. "More," she mouthed, being honest and clear about what she wanted, "give me more."

Adrian paused for but half a moment, gazing at Scarlett as if in wonder before giving her a hungry smile, all sharp, shining canines and flashing eyes. When he slammed into her Scarlett bit down on her lower lip in shock. When he did it again she reached up and bit into his shoulder, instead.

Adrian clung onto Scarlett even as she grabbed onto him, mercilessly kissing her with reckless abandon as he pounded into her. His breathing had grown even faster than Scarlett's.

When finally he let out a cry of pleasure, Adrian collapsed on top of Scarlett and buried his head against her neck, furling and unfurling his fingers through her hair as he kissed her skin.

"Thank you," he mumbled after a long moment, during which the only sounds had been the two of them regaining their breath and the ever-present crackle of the fire. "Thank you, thank you, thank you."

Scarlett glanced down at him, confused. "What for?"

"For letting this happen, of course," he laughed softly, somewhat incredulous. "That was...incredible. It shouldn't have been *that* good."

"Because I'm just an innocent little virgin, Mr Wolfe?"

Adrian bit into her neck before leaning up on his elbows to look at Scarlett. "Not anymore you're not, Red. Now you're mine."

She quirked an eyebrow. "Yours? I wasn't aware I

was anyone's but my own."

"You can be both. Just not anybody else's."

"So you're not going to run off never to be seen again now you got me into bed?"

Adrian let out a bark of laughter. "Hardly. You don't fuck a girl like that and not come back for more."

Scarlett swatted his cheek with her left hand. "Such foul language. I'm a lady, I'll have you know."

"I'm aware of that," he said, running his mouth down along Scarlett's chest to her stomach. He glanced up at her, grinning mischievously. "Which is why it's all the more satisfying to defile you, language and all."

Scarlett couldn't help but return the grin. She darted her eyes over to Adrian's clothes, which were still dripping wet. "It may take a few hours for those to dry. Do you have to be anywhere else this afternoon?"

"Please tell me that's an invitation to stay."

For a moment Scarlett considered that allowing Adrian to stay was madness. But she had just given her virginity to him; a few more hours of lying in bed with him was never going to bring it back.

She didn't *want* it back.

She wanted more of him.

Reaching a hand over to stroke Adrian's broken eyebrow, Scarlett nodded.

"Yes. Stay until your clothes are dry."

"And then?" Adrian asked from his position over her stomach. "What of tomorrow?"

She laughed. "Tomorrow is tomorrow. Let's just live for today."

He flashed another of his brilliant, maddeningly wicked smiles.

"I think I can agree to that."

CHAPTER TWENTY

Adrian

Never had Adrian felt so supremely satisfied with himself, even though he had spent the night curled up inside the hollow of a dead oak tree, as a wolf, in the middle of a storm. But now the storm had passed and the sun was shining through thousands of water droplets hanging from the branches above him, turning them to priceless jewels that glittered impossibly bright.

It was still cold - unseasonably so - but for once Adrian didn't care.

For he had slept with Scarlett Duke.

He had slept with Scarlett Duke not once, nor twice, nor even three times.

I don't think I've ever *been insatiable enough to go for five rounds in as many hours,* he mused as he finally reached the room he was renting in Mac's tavern, stripping off his cold, weather-beaten clothes and collapsing onto the bed with a thump. *I couldn't even bring myself to leave. I was cutting it rather fine with transforming.*

But Adrian didn't care that he had only made it out of Scarlett's bedroom, his clothes still uncomfortably damp, with fewer than ten minutes to spare before he turned into a wolf. Those same clothes had lain abandoned by his side as he hid from the storm for the night, useless and wretched but for the lingering smell of Scarlett that clung to them. For that reason Adrian had buried his snout in amongst the wet fabric, not caring for how the fibres scratched at his nose.

He was also too pleased with himself to worry about the fact that, sooner or later, he'd have to use his new-found relationship with Scarlett to get rid of his curse. In his current mindset that could be later, later, later, though deep inside himself Adrian knew it had to be sooner.

But that was something to dwell upon after a few hours of well-earned, warm and comfortable sleep. Adrian was exhausted after having spent so many successive nights as a wolf, since he didn't often sleep when in his lupine form. Added onto that his really rather active afternoon with Scarlett and Adrian was left feeling drained and empty.

Just a few hours of sleep and he'd be back to normal.

Just a few.

*

Adrian woke with a start, surprised by the darkness in his bedroom. The sun was already low in the sky, hidden by cloud. By Adrian's calculation he had less than an hour before it was time for him to transform once more. His heart sank.

I've wasted the entire day. I slept away all my freedom.

His skin tingled and ached with the mere thought of transforming. For a moment he considered fleeing Rowan and its woods – to find the exact boundary where Heidi Duke's curse couldn't hurt him. But it was too late for that; with less than an hour until he transformed Adrian would never make it out of the woods in time.

He banged his head repeatedly against the headboard.

"Fuck this, fuck this, fuck this," he muttered, over and over again, as if his words were themselves a curse. The ecstatic mood he'd been in before sleeping had thoroughly dissipated, leaving only the absolute knowledge that Adrian couldn't bear to spend another night as a wolf.

It had to stop. He was going insane.

It wasn't just because of the lack of sleep, or the fear, or the constant obsessing over how to get his curse removed that Adrian felt like he was going mad. With every night spent as a wolf he felt more and more of his human self being overwritten by far more animalistic, lupine urges. In all honesty Adrian didn't know how he managed to stay in Scarlett's room with the fire so close. If it hadn't been for what the two of them had been doing he wouldn't have been able to handle it.

Adrian had never been scared of fire before. Rather, he loved it, for the way his parents had used it to kill sickness and make food safe to eat and keep predators at bay.

But now he *was* the predator to be kept at bay, and becoming less and less like a human because of it.

He chuckled wryly at the thought. For, with regards to Scarlett, he was a different kind of predator to be protected from entirely.

She will never trust men again after I break her heart, Adrian thought, somewhat arrogantly. *But at least I won't be around to see that. I'll be on the other side of the world, somewhere warm and exotic and entirely devoid of wolves.*

Adrian used his remaining time as a human as best he could. He had food and hot water sent up so that he

182

could clean and eat. He shaved – for all the good that would do him as a wolf. He dressed in a finely made, loose white shirt with a forest green waistcoat delicately embroidered with gold. He paired them with green leggings so dark they were almost black, a supple pair of brown leather, thigh high boots and a jacket embroidered in much the same way as the waistcoat. He finished off the look with one, solitary gold earring in his left ear.

Even just for his remaining ten minutes Adrian wanted to look at himself in the mirror and see the man he could have been if not for the fact he turned into a wolf. The man he could still be, once the curse was lifted.

Except he would have little soul left to his name, and his heart would belong to Scarlett Duke.

My freedom for my heart is not too bad a price, Adrian thought bitterly as he watched his reflection frown, his split eyebrow appearing even more pronounced because of it. He ran a hand through his hair, pushing back the white. It was getting too long. Once he was free of Rowan – free of Heidi Duke – he'd have it cut.

And then he waited. Waited for the insufferable, agonising cracks of his bones that told Adrian he had to remove his clothes and prepare to transform.

The feeling never came.

For over an hour he waited. Two. For one wild moment he considered whether Heidi had simply given up. But that didn't seem possible in the slightest; he knew her too well. He looked out of the window in his room, hoping for an explanation.

And then he saw it – or, rather, *didn't.*

There was no moon in the sky.

"The new moon," Adrian murmured, lips curling up into a delighted grin. He had never thought about the limitations of his curse, since Heidi could extend it past the full moon as and when she pleased.

Clearly he had found the limit.

Wasting no time, though he knew it was foolish, Adrian grabbed his cloak, since he had not been outside at night as a human for weeks and didn't want to be surprised by how cold the air could get. He raced down the stairs and out of Mac's tavern, making a beeline for the woods and the little house nestled inside where all his troubles lay. Even though Heidi Duke would be in – even though Samuel Birch might be there – Adrian didn't care.

If this was his only opportunity to have one night with Scarlett then he would take it. One whole night, to watch her under the light of the stars through human eyes. To touch her with human fingers. To speak to her with words understandable to human ears.

He would take it. It would be a memory he'd cling to after he destroyed one of the best things that had happened to him in a long, long time.

When he reached the edge of the trees surrounding the house Adrian slowed. He could see Heidi sitting in the kitchen, drinking tea and working with what looked like straw. On any other night he'd care about what the witch was up to, but not tonight.

He stalked carefully around to Scarlett's window, painfully aware of every noise he made that he could avoid making as a wolf. But he was much quieter than an ordinary human, and he knew where he was going.

Scarlett wasn't in her room, but Adrian didn't care. With skill he slipped a pin through the crack in her window and undid the latch from the outside. He manoeuvred through, landing on the floor with barely a sound at all. Closing the window behind him, Adrian considered what to do until Scarlett returned.

Outside the door, which lay ajar, Adrian could hear the woman in question talking to someone. Sam. He crept closer to eavesdrop.

"What do you mean there's something different about me, Sam? I'm exactly the same."

"But you're not! You're –"

"Happier?"

"I...yes. Sort of."

"And that's a bad thing?"

Sam sighed heavily; Adrian grinned.

You poor boy, he thought. *I know what it is you want to say. But will you say it?*

"You're distracted," Sam finally said. "And people have seen you conversing with Mister Wolfe far more often than you used to. Are the two of you –"

"Don't ask me about Adrian, Sam."

Adrian liked that she used his first name when talking about him to other people. It had taken him long enough to get her to use it, after all. With a pang he realised she would be loathe ever to think his name in a few days, much less utter it. He shook the thought away.

A glint of silver from Scarlett's dressing table caught his eye. Distracted, Adrian wandered away from the conversation to inspect it. It was a snowdrop, perfectly recreated in pure, solid silver. It was impossibly delicate. It was beautiful.

Adrian knew who had made it. After watching the man hand over real snowdrops to Scarlett when he proposed, it was obvious. He had to hand it to Jakob Schmidt – he was certainly a master of his craft. Picking the flower up Adrian thought that, maybe once Scarlett had gotten over his betrayal, she might find happiness with the blacksmith. He didn't seem like a bad man, and was certainly far more Scarlett's type than Sam was.

A few more seconds of staring at the entrancing piece of craft work in his hands and Adrian had an idea. Glancing at the door to ensure nobody was coming through, he pulled out a tiny vial of startlingly blue, viscous liquid. Adrian unstoppered it, tilting the bottle until three individual drops of the stuff fell onto the head of the snowdrop.

"Let no curse nor spell nor potion ever affect the person to whom this was gifted," Adrian whispered, very careful with his words. For a person could steal the snowdrop, or break it into pieces, or throw it away, but that could never change the fact that Jakob had given it to Scarlett. So long as even a piece of it existed on this earth then Scarlett would be protected.

From her grandmother, Adrian thought. *From me. Let this be my own gift to you, Scarlett.*

Adrian replaced the snowdrop onto the dressing table when he heard a creak at the door. Hiding behind her wardrobe he waited until Scarlett appeared, closing the door behind her. Then he crept up on her, holding a hand over her mouth when she gasped in shock.

"Shh," he murmured into her ear. "It's me. It's Adrian."

Scarlett's eyes went wide as Adrian let go of her mouth and allowed her to turn around.

"What are you doing here?" she asked, keeping her voice quiet. Scarlett headed over to the window and closed the curtains, then slid a bolt across the door.

"Why else would I have crept into your room other than to see you, Scarlett?"

Adrian was satisfied to see a small, delighted smile curl her beautiful lips.

Face flushed, she whispered, "Would you like to spend the night, Adrian?"

His mouth on hers was all the answer Adrian needed to give.

One night, he thought. *We can have one whole night.*

For after that everything would change.

CHAPTER TWENTY-ONE

Scarlett

When Scarlett woke it was with shock and delight that she wasn't alone. Adrian was still asleep, softly breathing away his white lock of hair whenever it fell across his face. She glanced down; he was holding her hand.

When did that happen? Scarlett thought as she blushed. *Have we been holding hands the entire time we were asleep?*

Not that the two of them spent much of the night

sleeping in the first place. Though they'd had to keep as silent as a wolf stalking through the night so that her grandmother wouldn't know Scarlett was anything but alone in her room, the act of keeping things secret only seemed to make them hungrier for each other.

Scarlett's body ached from it. But it was a satisfying ache – proof that what she and Adrian were doing was real. That they truly wanted each other.

She still struggled to believe it nonetheless.

Reaching out a hand, Scarlett dared to touch the gold earring Adrian was wearing on his left ear. It was the *only* thing he was wearing. Though the man was always vain and immaculately dressed to a fault, Scarlett had never seen him wear jewellery before. She wondered why.

The touch of his earring turned into Scarlett stroking back his soft, jet-black hair. It still surprised her how silky it was. She intertwined her fingers through it, revelling in the feeling of allowing herself to touch Adrian in the first place.

His amber eyes sprung open.

"Morning," he murmured sleepily. His mouth curved into the laziest of smiles as he reached up a hand to envelop the one Scarlett had running through his hair. "Sleep well?"

"When I slept, yes."

He snickered. "Well put. I suppose I should run off

before your grandmother checks to see if you're awake."

Scarlett couldn't help feeling crestfallen, though she knew Adrian was correct. With a sigh she tried to pull her hand away from his – the hands that had stayed clasped together all night – but Adrian merely held on tighter.

Pulling her against his chest, he sank his face into Scarlett's hair and hitched a leg around one of hers, only entangling them further.

"Adrian, what are you doing?" Scarlett whispered, though she didn't want him to stop. Before she found the sense to resist the urge she planted kisses along his collarbone and up his neck, whilst running a gentle hand down his spine.

Adrian shivered contentedly like a cat getting stroked. He bent his head until his lips found Scarlett's; they were slightly chapped just as, Scarlett realised, her own were. She was parched. But to get a cup of water was to break the magic of being in bed with Adrian, so she ignored her thirst.

They kissed for as long as they dared – deep, lingering kisses that spoke of the night they'd just shared. But the sun was only creeping further and further across the floor of Scarlett's room through a gap in the curtain. Outside, the chatter of larks and wrens and thrushes was filling the morning air. They grew ever more insistent as the seconds passed.

Breathless and tingling, Scarlett forced herself to push Adrian away. "You need to go."

He kissed the tip of her nose. "I know. That doesn't mean either of us wants me to."

If their faces weren't a mere inch from each other Scarlett may well have looked away at the candid remark. It felt *wrong* to want to stay in bed all day, naked and hot and twisted around Adrian Wolfe.

But she wanted it. She wanted it more than anything.

"I'll see you when I come into market in a couple of hours," she said as Adrian finally, regretfully, rolled out of her bed.

"Would you like to eat with me at midday?"

Scarlett blinked in surprise. She sat up, clutching at the sheets to protect her modesty despite the fact Adrian had only just been in bed with her.

He laughed softly at the expression on her face. He pulled on his shirt and leggings, sliding into his boots before putting on his beautifully embroidered waistcoat. "Unless my lady doesn't have an appetite, or is trying to find a polite way to tell me to leave her alone."

"No, I'd love to!" Scarlett announced quickly, and possibly a little too loudly. "I was just...surprised, I suppose?"

Adrian raised an eyebrow. "How so?"

"It just seems like an altogether gentlemanly thing to do. Like you're courting me properly."

"I *am* a gentleman, and I *am* courting you properly."

She glanced at the bed pointedly. "Most courtships I know of don't involve climbing into bed together before at least a proposal for marriage is made."

"But I do not wish to be married, and neither do you. In which case surely I have courted you properly?"

Scarlett rolled her eyes, but she let out a small laugh. "Clearly I cannot hope to win against your infallible logic, Adrian."

He grinned. "Wonderful."

As he was reaching for his cloak, peeping out the window trying to determine if he would actually need to put it on, Scarlett couldn't help but appreciate how handsome the man was, especially in his green-and-gold attire.

"I can see you watching me in the window, Scarlett," Adrian said with a smirk.

She blushed. "I'm allowed to look, aren't I?"

"Far more than that, I should think."

"You look particularly dashing today. Those clothes –"

"Were the last gift my parents gave me. Or, rather, were planning to," Adrian explained. "They had them stored away for my twenty-first birthday. But then they died. I haven't worn them before."

"But you've carried them with you wherever you go since then?"

Adrian nodded. He continued to watch Scarlett watching him through the reflection on the window. It kept his own face somewhat obscured from Scarlett, so she couldn't see his expression properly. But the set of his shoulders seemed distant and deeply sad, so Scarlett crept out of bed despite her nakedness and went to him.

When she reached Adrian's side he turned to face her, though the look on his face was carefully crafted and neutral.

"You miss them," she said. It wasn't a question.

"Of course I do. But missing them won't bring them back."

It hurt Scarlett to hear this, though of course it was true. She wrapped her arms around Adrian and leant her head against his chest; his heart was beating quickly. Quicker than Scarlett's.

"You're not alone, you know," she mumbled. "Or, at least, you don't have to be."

Adrian was silent. When Scarlett looked up his eyes seemed just a little too glassy. But then he blinked, and they were fine.

He smiled at her. "I'll see you in a few hours, Miss

Scarlett."

And then he kissed her lips, and then he was gone.

*

Adrian's idea of eating at midday was to not open his stall, sweep Scarlett onto his arm the moment she arrived at market and demand her attention for the entire day, under the gawking, disbelieving eyes of everyone in Rowan.

Scarlett saw Charlie, who realised there and then that he'd never be able to compete with a man like Adrian Wolfe. She saw Jakob, who roared with understanding laughter when he caught sight of the pair of them. He shook his head in amusement and despair. Scarlett stuck her tongue out at him.

She hoped he would take that as her way of saying: this isn't serious. I'm only having fun.

Scarlett didn't believe her own lie for a second.

For how could she? It had taken everything in her to resist Adrian's charms, and now she had given in and fallen for them. She was in too deep and she knew it. If the man asked her to run off with her in the dark of night she'd say yes in a heartbeat without even blinking.

It would be the wrong choice.

She'd make it anyway.

To that end she knew she had to be careful. But

Adrian's arm was around her waist, or clasping her hand, or weaving flowers into her hair as he commented on the people watching them in typically witty, almost cruel fashion.

When finally the sun dipped low into the sky, Adrian settled her onto a bench whilst he entered Mac's tavern for food and drink. He didn't want to go inside with Scarlett, where everybody else was. He wanted her to himself.

Scarlett only felt herself falling even harder for Adrian with every passing moment. The last two days had been like a dream. She didn't want to wake up, though she knew at some point she needed to.

But not right now.

"Scarlett?"

Scarlett looked up at who had spoken; it wasn't Adrian.

Andreas Sommer stood there, a frown upon his perfectly elegant face. "Scarlett, what are you doing?" he asked when Scarlett continued to look at him instead of answering.

"I'm sitting on a bench, Andreas," she said, pointing out the obvious.

"You know what I mean. What are you doing with *him?*"

He gestured towards Adrian as he left the tavern and

made a beeline towards Scarlett. The easy-going smile on his face immediately fell away when he saw Andreas.

Scarlett didn't like the way Andreas was talking to her, not at all. She stood up.

"What is that you're insinuating, Andreas? Is there something wrong with me enjoying Mr Wolfe's company?"

He grimaced when Adrian reached the two of them. "Can you leave us alone? I'm clearly speaking with Miss Scarlett in -"

"Whatever it is you want to say to me regarding Adrian Wolfe can be said in front of the man in question," Scarlett interrupted, ensuring that her face remained bland and genial even as her words were pointed and accusatory.

Andreas seemed to flounder. Adrian half-smirked at the look on the man's face.

"Go on, Andreas Sommer," he said. "What is so wrong with Miss Scarlett spending time with me that you felt it prudent to interrupt it?"

"You know fine well what's wrong with it!" Andreas finally exploded. He looked at Scarlett. "You're better than this. You're better than *him*. Don't damage your future more than you already have by wasting more time on him."

"Excuse me?" Scarlett spoke these words in a quiet,

controlled rage. She took a step towards Andreas and pushed him away. "And who are you to tell me this? Nobody has the right to tell me what to do or who to see, Andreas. Especially not a classist, entitled man whose proposal to marry me merely involved the fact that our fathers would like it if we did. I'm not a chess piece, and I'm not your mild-natured future wife, either. So go away, and leave us alone."

Both Andreas and Adrian stared at her, stunned by the outburst. For a moment it looked as if Andreas might say something. But then, after spending far too long saying nothing, he scowled at the two of them and stalked away.

Scarlett let out a large *whoosh* of air. She laughed an uncertain laugh as she caught Adrian's eye. "I can't believe I just said that."

"Neither can I. Will there be repercussions for you saying that to him?"

"If there are, I don't care. Either I'm a nobody and it doesn't matter, or I'm a Duke and it matters even less."

Adrian's gazed at her in wonder. "That almost sounds arrogant enough that I would say it."

Scarlett shrugged, though in truth she was very pleased with Adrian saying that. "Is it arrogant if it's true? I suppose that doesn't matter, either."

He placed the food and drink he'd retrieved from the tavern down on the bench. Then, with an overwhelming tenderness that Scarlett had not yet experienced from the man, Adrian stroked the side of her cheek with an ungloved hand and just barely brushed his lips against hers.

But his expression was regretful. Scarlett didn't like that at all.

"Adrian –"

"You're going to hate me, but I have to go. Take the food back for your grandmother. Or Sam. I'm sure he'll see it as a peace offering after you told him off last night."

Scarlett's cheeks burned. "You heard all that?"

"Just a little. He's simply being jealous and protective. I would be, too, if I were pining for you and lost you to another man. I don't think there's any need to be so harsh with him."

She sighed, looking down at the ground before returning to stare into Adrian's sorrowful amber eyes. "I guess not," she mumbled. "Must you go *now*?"

He nodded. "You'll get home safe?"

"It's not time for the wolves to be in our neck of the woods yet. I'll be fine."

Adrian laughed at this. It was unexpected. It felt entirely out of place.

"I suppose they're *not* in the woods right now, are they? Of course they're not."

"Adrian?"

He kissed her again.

"Be off before it gets too dark. Give my regards to little Sam...I'm sure he'll appreciate it."

And then he left for Mac's tavern, where his room was. Scarlett picked up the basket laden with food and drink, numbly making her way out of Rowan and through the woods without really thinking about where she was going.

I have to go.

An uncomfortable feeling of dread washed over Scarlett when she realised Adrian did not say for how long.

CHAPTER TWENTY-TWO

Adrian

It took everything in Adrian's power to head to Heidi Duke's house when he was sure Scarlett was in Rowan. His night spent as a wolf had been exhausting. Even if he'd wanted to sleep he wouldn't have been able to.

All he could think of was Scarlett, and how he would betray her, and how much he didn't want to.

But it was taking him longer and longer to feel human again after transforming. If he took much more of this curse he'd lose himself altogether. He had to put himself first.

He *had* to.

Adrian glanced through the kitchen window of the house first. Three straw dolls lay on the table, one larger than the other two. It seemed as if Heidi was beginning to give them features. Also on the table lay a few bottles. One of them Adrian recognised as the concentrated hemlock he'd handed over to Scarlett to give to the old woman. It didn't inspire in him much hope that what was in the other bottles was anything more pleasant than that.

He didn't like the look of what she was doing at all.

But it wasn't his problem anymore. A knock on the door, a threat and a bargain or two, and Adrian would be done. He'd be gone.

And he'd never see Scarlett again.

Adrian hated how torn he was on the matter. It wasn't like him at all. But when he thought about how Scarlett had defended him in front of Andreas – how she had spent all day with him under the judgemental scrutiny of the entire town of Rowan, and how her father must surely now know about what she was up to – all he wanted to do was find her and kiss her until she was aching for him.

He forced the painfully tantalising thought away. For his own good he buried it deep inside.

He knocked on the door.

"Who is it?" Heidi asked in a quavering, old lady voice that wasn't how she ever spoke to Adrian at all.

"Your grand-daughter," he joked humourlessly.

He knew she was frowning, trying to work out who it really was. "Is that you, Adrian Wolfe?" she eventually asked.

"A wolf indeed. May I come in?"

"Let yourself in," she said, irritated, reverting to her true, harsh voice in an instant.

When Adrian opened the door he saw that Heidi was making tea over the fire. She glowered at Adrian. "What do you want? I'm busy."

"Clearly. I won't be long."

Adrian took in the contents on the table, eyeing them a little more suspiciously than before. But he didn't let on his misgivings.

He smiled easily. "Straw dolls. Working up a bit of long-distance magic, I see."

Heidi scowled. "My business is my own. What do you want?"

He resisted taking in a steady breath. "I slept with your grand-daughter. Many times. One might say I'm courting her. Doubtless word would have reached your ears eventually."

It felt as if the atmosphere in the room had frozen,

though the fire Adrian kept well away from was roaring merrily.

"Leave her alone."

"Ah, see, that is why I am here. Lift my curse. Leave *me* alone, and I'll leave her alone."

"Give me one good reason why I shouldn't send your soul to hell and curse your useless corpse for a thousand years."

Adrian laughed at the threat, which he knew she could well make good on. "Come now, Heidi; no need to go to such extremes. And besides," Adrian put on his easiest smile, knowing he was lying, "if you do something to me Scarlett will know it was you."

Heidi looked torn between outrage and horror. "And what makes you say that? What have you told her?"

"Oh, nothing that would worry you...if you lift my curse. It will only matter if you don't."

Adrian was skilled with magic and curses and poisons too, of course, so Heidi daren't think his words an idle threat.

"She cares for you, doesn't she?" Heidi eventually said after a long silence. "Samuel was right; she's been different lately. It's because of you."

Adrian said nothing.

"Have you no heart?" the old lady continued,

walking away from the fire to round on Adrian. "She is barely an adult. Just a child, really. Can you really be so cruel?"

"As I recall, I was *barely an adult* when you cursed me, witch. Now undo it, then you and Scarlett shall never see me again. If you don't then I'll keep courting her. I'll make her run off with me, until she's simply mad for me, and when she does I'll tell her all about you and she will believe every word I say. You will lose her. And then I'll break her heart, and you won't be able to comfort her."

Heidi seemed torn. To lift his curse would mean she lost to Adrian, but to do nothing would mean to lose Scarlett.

Adrian gave her the illusion of choice by granting her some time to think. He wandered over to the table, inspecting the straw dolls once more. It seemed as if the tallest was a woman, with a pretty, painted face; the other two, her children. The details – braces holding their trousers up, freckles, toothy grins – gave off the distinct impression that they were boys. They were identical. Twins.

Twins.

It took Adrian but a second to work out what was going on. The dolls were Scarlett's step-mother and her brothers.

What were their names? Rudy and...Elias. Rudy and Elias. And their mother, Frances.

Adrian had never performed such magic before, but he knew how it went. Stab the dolls with pins, or break their legs, or set them on fire, and the same fate will be dealt to the individual whose likeness the maker has used. Soak the dolls in poison, and...

"You know what?" Adrian said, struggling to keep his voice calm. "You have until tomorrow to decide. I can see this is a tough decision you must make."

We'll run away, he thought, forming the best plan he could possibly think of on the spot. *Me and Scarlett. She'll come with me. She'll leave and she'll never know what her grandmother does to her family. It doesn't matter than I'm a wolf sometimes. I can live with that. I've lived with it for six years.*

Heidi seemed distracted. She scowled. "What, so you can crawl into my grand-daughter's bed? I think not."

"It's to pack my stall, actually. One way or another it won't be returning to Rowan. There are some things packed inside I'd rather the townspeople didn't get their hands on."

For a moment it looked like Heidi would refuse. But then she waved him off. "Fine. *Fine.* But you don't have until tomorrow. Come back just before sunset. We will make our deal then...one way or the other."

Adrian nodded, heart hammering in his chest as he headed for the open door and saw –

"Adrian?" Scarlett said in confusion. "Nana, what's going on?"

"*Run,*" was all Adrian said, making to grab Scarlett as he tried to flee. But Scarlett stood glued to the spot.

"What is going on?"

"Oh, Red, you must send this man away!" Heidi wailed, back to sounding old and defenceless and terrified. Adrian noticed that she'd swept the dolls and poisons away. "He has been threatening me, telling me the most awful things!"

Scarlett darted her eyes from Adrian to her grandmother, suspicious. She pulled her arm out of Adrian's grasp.

Oh, no.

"Scarlett, don't listen to her –"

"He told me he's planning on breaking your heart to get back at me! Oh, Red, he's awful!"

"I – what?"

"He tried to con me six years ago, and I caught him out on his lie, and he's been holding a grudge ever since! He was playing with you this whole time, intent on ruining you just to get back at me. A petty, selfish man if ever I saw one. I should have known."

Scarlett froze. Her face grew pale. She looked at Adrian.

"Tell me this isn't true."

"Scarlett, please, just get out of here and I'll explain. Your grandmother –"

"Is it true?!"

"Yes!" he cried out despite himself. He could feel bile and panic rising equally in his throat. Everything was going wrong. "Yes, but not really. Just let me –"

"Get out."

"Scarlett –"

"*Get out*!"

"But she's trying to –"

"I don't want to hear another word coming out of your mouth!" Scarlett howled, her face twisted in betrayal. "I don't want you near me. I was right to doubt you. I should have trusted my instincts. Look where ignoring them got me!"

He reached out for her; Scarlett backed away. Out of the corner of his eye Adrian saw Heidi grinning maliciously at him.

Adrian had lost. He had lost so much more than he thought he was capable of losing.

Scarlett's eyes were bright and shining with angry, vicious tears. "Get out," she uttered once more, her voice quiet and barely controlled. "Get out of this house. Get out of Rowan. Don't let me see you again."

He left.

On his way out he saw Sam, who had clearly been listening to everything from the garden. It looked like the man wanted to punch him.

"Look after her," Adrian muttered quickly, too quietly for Scarlett or her grandmother to hear. "Sam, *watch* out for her. In there."

His ambiguous warning left Sam too stunned to hit him, as he'd wanted.

Adrian ran off before he did something stupid, like heading back inside the house and trying to drag Scarlett out against her will. With Sam and Heidi there he'd never manage it.

But as he ran, numb and horrified on human legs, a thought that had never once crossed his mind before started screaming at him.

I wish I was a wolf, it said. *A thoughtless, unfeeling wolf who could tear an old woman to shreds and flee off into the darkness.*

But Adrian was not a wolf.

He was merely a man.

CHAPTER TWENTY-THREE

Scarlett

Scarlett cried for a long time that afternoon. She cried for a long time that night. She cried for a long time the next morning and well past lunchtime even then.

It was only when evening fell the following day that Scarlett's tears finally dried up, leaving her head pounding, her eyes swollen and her heart crushed to a fine powder.

She should never have let this happen. She should never have taken a walk into the woods with a man like

Mister Wolfe.

But Scarlett had, and now she didn't know what to do.

She was beyond furious with herself. *How many times did I try to stop myself? How many times did I say it wasn't a good idea? That I'd get hurt? And yet I didn't listen,* she thought, over and over again. She had shied away from everybody else's advice, thinking herself clever enough to make her own decisions.

But no, she wasn't clever. The only clever one was scheming, lying, heartbreaking Adrian Wolfe.

Her grandmother had called it correctly – he was petty. He'd clearly been thinking about using Scarlett to get back at her grandmother for a while. He had told Scarlett he'd been watching her since the fateful night he saved her in the woods. That he'd wanted her. She'd taken it as flattery. As desire.

And he had taken her for a fool.

Miserably she felt her eyes sting with new tears, though her eyes were too painful to bear them. She flung herself against the pillow, rubbing her face against the fabric even as she willed herself to stop existing entirely.

Scarlett's stomach grumbled and bit at her insides, reminding her that she hadn't eaten since the morning before and was starving. She felt too sick to eat. Too furious.

Too heartbroken.

For the only reason it hurt so much to have Adrian betray her like this was because Scarlett truly had fallen for him. She had known it for a while, from the moment she gave in and let him kiss her in the woods. She had known it, she had tried to ignore it, and then she gave in. It was all her own fault she had fallen for Adrian's con.

She wondered how much of his family history was true, if any. Were his parents even dead? Was his village overwrought by disease that only he survived? Thinking on it now it seemed so unlikely. Adrian had even told her his father was a con-man and that he'd taken that up.

Scarlett should have heeded that as the warning that it was: *do not trust this man. Ignore him. Push him away.*

"Miss Scarlett?" Sam's voice asked uncertainly, muffled by the heavy wood of the door as he knocked upon it.

"Go away," she tried to call back, but her voice was hoarse and cracked from disuse. She was so thirsty. It reminded her, unbidden, of how thirsty she'd been only two mornings before, when she was still in the arms of Adrian Wolfe. Thirsty for water and thirsty for him.

And now he was gone, and Scarlett felt like she was drowning in her own naivety.

"Miss Scarlett, you need to eat. At least let me bring you some water."

Scarlett saw the sense in this. She did not want to die, though she felt like she had died from shame a hundred times over already. So she nodded at the door on reflex before saying, "Fine."

Sam was carrying a tray laden with toasted bread and a selection of meats and cheeses. There was a bowl of broth, too, as well as a wooden cup filled with water and a steaming mug of tea. He brought it over and placed it on her bedside table; Scarlett picked up the water immediately, drank it in one go, then gingerly picked up the bowl of broth and cradled its warmth in her hands.

"Thank you," she eventually said to Sam, remembering her manners. He stared at her awkwardly, his shoulders stooped slightly despite the fact the ceiling was high enough for him to stand up straight. Scarlett couldn't bear to have him see her like this – not after Sam had tried to warn her away from the man responsible for causing her anguish.

"Miss Scarlett –"

"Please, Sam, I don't want to hear it," she interrupted, knowing that if she was forced to talk about what happened she'd start crying again.

"I – I didn't want to tell you I told you so or anything," he said, head drooping sadly. "I just wanted to ask how you are."

"I think that's fairly obvious."

"This isn't your fault, Scarlett."

"It is, and you know it," she snapped. "Don't you dare take away my responsibility for my own actions. I did what I did. I'll face up to it myself."

Sam seemed torn. He desperately wanted to comfort Scarlett but it was clear that she wasn't going to listen to anything he said.

He sighed heavily and headed for the door. "Okay, Miss Scarlett. Sorry to bother you."

"Oh Sam, no -" Scarlett called out, feeling immediately terrible about treating him so appallingly. "I'm the one who's sorry. I just need to wallow in it for a bit. Thank you for the food."

She managed just the barest of smiles in his direction. It didn't meet her red, teary eyes, but it was enough. Sam returned the smile, nodded his head, then left Scarlett's bedroom, closing the door behind him.

Scarlett collapsed against her pillow. She had no appetite for the soup in her hands but knew she had to drink it. And so slowly, agonisingly, she gulped the lot down, cleaning the sides of the bowl with a hunk of bread which she forced down her throat. She ignored the meat and cheese. By the time she was finished eating the tea had gone tepid, so she left it untouched, too.

Then she heard a noise outside, and Scarlett's head snapped immediately to the window.

A pair of wolf eyes stared back, amber and gold and so infuriatingly like Adrian's that she couldn't bear it.

The wolf whined when Scarlett's face twisted in fury.

"Go away!" she yelled, picking up the mug of tea and launching it at the window. It exploded against the glass, startling the wolf away with a swish of its tail and barely a look back over its shoulder at Scarlett.

But it didn't make her feel better.

No. All it left Scarlett was alone, with cold tea seeping into the floor like a poisonous curse.

She didn't care.

CHAPTER TWENTY-FOUR

Adrian

Close to two weeks had passed since Scarlett threw her tea at her window and chased away Adrian as a wolf. He had hoped she wouldn't. He had hoped that, even in the form he hated more than anything, he could stay close to her.

But she had yelled him away.

Adrian had packed up his stall and hidden all of his belongings deep in the woods, where Scarlett nor any other passerby would ever dare to tread. He had paid his bill for the room he'd barely used in Mac's tavern.

And then he'd left Rowan and its damnable forest until he could be sure he was out of reach of Heidi's curse.

The relief of seeing the moon with his own eyes was overwhelming, even though he had so desperately, viciously wished to be a wolf the day Heidi had outmanoeuvred him. He spent a few days in the nearest village, sleeping away most of his time in order to catch up on the hours he had lost. The rest of the time he merely lay there and mulled over what to do.

His original instinct to grab Scarlett and flee had been wrong. She would have found out what happened to her family and she would be distraught. She would hate him. She'd never want to see him again.

But most of all, Scarlett would lose her brothers and her step-mother, and Adrian wouldn't be able to live with that.

So it was without any sort of plan whatsoever that he warily crept back into the woods of Rowan. That night, however, he did not transform.

Good, he thought with some satisfaction. *Heidi has at least reverted my curse to what it was. Or is not aware that I am back.*

But the full moon was approaching; by his measure Adrian had just four days before he would have to transform for three nights, following the rules of his original curse. That didn't leave him much time at all, given that Scarlett would not listen to him if he were to approach her in public, and whilst she was in her grandmother's house or with Sam he couldn't speak to her, either.

Which left grabbing hold of her when she walked through the woods, alone.

Just like how we first met, he thought wryly.

And then...then he'd have to hope Scarlett believed him. He had no idea what to do.

It was with some surprise that Adrian found himself hiding in the tree-line by Heidi Duke's house. He knew he couldn't stop her right now, unprepared as he was. The best Adrian would be able to do is to try and prepare a curse or spell from what he had in his hidden, packed away stall, but until he was sure he had stopped what the woman was planning to do to Scarlett's family then Adrian's hand was stayed.

Adrian noticed, then, that he wasn't entirely alone. For Sam was in the garden, though he wasn't paying attention to what he was doing – he had been digging the same patch of earth over and over for at least five minutes. No, he was carefully watching Heidi Duke through the window, which was ajar.

Good on you, Sam! Adrian felt like whooping. Clearly the boy was smarter than Adrian had ever given him credit for.

It seemed as if Heidi was humming or singing or talking to herself, for Sam's face was scrunched up in concentration as he listened to what she said. Adrian couldn't hear, but by the growing horror creeping into Sam's face he realised it wasn't anything good. But it was what Adrian needed him to hear.

Sam's complexion had gone pale and sickly, as if he might throw up, when he spied Adrian in his hiding spot. He froze immediately; what would Sam do now? The young man mouthed silent, slow words at him, over and over again until Adrian worked out what he was trying to say.

What do we do?

Adrian ushered him over with a wave of his hand. But Sam was in such a rush to comply – so relieved to be told what to do – that he knocked over a bucket and tripped on the long handle of a shovel as he tried to exit the garden. He made it halfway to Adrian when Heidi appeared at the front door.

Adrian only just managed to conceal himself behind the trees, though he felt like a wretched coward leaving Sam alone.

"Samuel, I didn't realise you were here," Heidi said, her voice sickly sweet and sing-song.

Adrian didn't have to see Sam to know what kind of face he was making. "I was j-just finishing up, m-ma'am," he stuttered. "I'm going to head back to my father's mill,

219

now. He needs me this afternoon."

But Sam knew he wasn't going to be leaving, just as surely as Adrian and Heidi knew. Adrian's stomach twisted in trepidation as Heidi laughed.

"Oh, I don't think so, dear," she said. "Going by your face you heard me singing to the dolls. Magic is such vocal work, you see. I can never do it when Red is around. Or you. I thought I had been so careful." She sighed heavily. "I was fond of you, Sam. But I won't let you tell Scarlett, and I know you will."

Sam bolted. In the opposite direction of Adrian he bolted, straight through the trees.

But Heidi was already weaving her words into a spell, and with a silvery pulse of light the hurried, frightened sound of Sam's footsteps disappeared without a trace.

Humming to herself in satisfaction, Heidi returned to her house without checking to see what had become of Sam. But Adrian wanted to know. He hadn't recognised her spell, after all. And if Sam were dead then Heidi would have taken care of the body, to ensure Scarlett didn't find him.

Which meant he was alive...in one form or another.

Adrian stalked through the trees until he reached where he'd seen the light originate from. He didn't need to search to find where Sam had gone or what had become of him.

For Sam stood in front of him, broad and tall and strong as he always had been.

Except, now, it wasn't just Adrian Wolfe who lived up to his namesake.

Heidi had turned Sam into a birch tree.

Adrian wanted to laugh in sickening, frightening glee, as if he had lost his wits entirely, but he held it back with a hand across his mouth as if keeping in bile.

We're doomed, he thought as he collapsed against the silver tree that was Sam, and cried. Adrian hadn't wept in years.

"I always thought I'd cry over a woman," he whispered to the tree, not knowing nor caring if it could hear him. "Not over a miller's boy. Though I guess I'm doing both."

He didn't know what to do. Adrian had no plan, no allies, and, increasingly, no time. He needed something – some irrefutable proof – to show Scarlett, to make her believe in everything Adrian told her. He glared up at the sun glaring back at him in the sky. Even though it was May it still held little heat, as if it were reflecting the current state of Adrian's heart.

But then it struck him, looking up there in the sky. Something so ridiculous that even Scarlett would be forced to listen to him after witnessing it.

It would be full in four days.

The moon.

CHAPTER TWENTY-FIVE

Scarlett

Scarlett felt akin to a zombie two weeks after Adrian had betrayed her. She had no tears left to cry. She had no feelings left at all. She was hollow. She was nothing.

That was when her father sent for her to visit the Duke house, and Scarlett's heart dared to stir back to life. If she could be welcomed back into the family – despite her shame – then Scarlett would be sure never to feel sorrowful again. And she would listen to her father, and Frances, and Sam, and everyone else who only ever had her best interests at heart. Even Andreas, who may simply have wanted Scarlett to stay away from Adrian Wolfe for being, well, Adrian Wolfe.

She put on the red dress. The one she had fled to her grandmother's house in. The one she'd been wearing when she ran into Adrian's arms. It was symbolic; if Scarlett was allowed back into the family then she would burn it to ashes and be glad of it. And if not...

Let's not think of 'if not'.

She wrapped herself up in her grandmother's cloak and kept her long hair loose and wavy around her face, to help hide her slightly hollowed cheeks that were proof she still wasn't eating properly, even two weeks later. Sam hadn't even been around for the last few days, with a gentle smile and a plea for her to look after herself. For he had fallen ill, her grandmother told her, which made Scarlett feel even worse for the distant way she had been treating Sam lately.

When he returns, Scarlett decided, *I will think of him better. I will treat him better, like he has always treated me.*

Scarlett's grandmother had been preoccupied recently – almost as much as Scarlett herself had been preoccupied with infuriating thoughts of Adrian. Perhaps she was deliberately leaving Scarlett alone, since she was determined that Scarlett should be strong and get over the folly of falling for a con-man all on her own.

Scarlett knew her grandmother was right. And it was

224

what she planned to do – what she was *trying* to do. She just never knew it would be so hard.

She hadn't wanted to fall in love with anyone.

She had, anyway.

It was with a stomach sick with nerves that Scarlett stepped out of the carriage her father had sent for her and allowed a servant to see her through the ornate front doors and into the main body of the house. These weren't the doors she had run out from, two years ago – she had used the side door by the study – but it felt symbolic nonetheless to finally be welcomed back through the threshold of a house she had been shunned from for so long.

Scarlett was desperate that this would not be the last time she was allowed in.

The air in the house was far more serious than she had expected. Even the staff seemed in a far more stately mood than usual. And she was shown up to her parents' bedroom, rather than the parlour or her father's study. A horrible sense of dread began to creep over Scarlett; part of her wished to flee and run back out of the house.

But she stayed, and she was let into the room.

And there, helplessly pale and feverish in the large bed, laid Frances, Rudy and Elias, who were curled against their mother's arms. Her father sat in a chair by the bed, watching on helplessly with overly bright eyes.

"Papa –" Scarlett barely let out before he began to cry at the sight of her, rushing over and embracing his only daughter with shaking arms that did not seem to want to let her go.

"My love," he wept against her hair. "You came, you came. Rudy, Elias – look who's here!"

He pulled away from Scarlett so that she could tiptoe over to the bed. All three of its inhabitants seemed delirious, but upon noticing her presence both boys seemed to light up.

"Sister," Rudy said, his voice rattling, his breathing laboured.

"...missed you," Elias moaned, clearly in pain.

Scarlett sobbed. She couldn't stop it; the cries choked and clawed at her throat until she allowed them out. She reached out a hand to each of her brothers. When they tried and failed to grab hold of her fingers she only cried harder.

And then another voice spoke.

"Scarlett," Frances called out weakly, her voice barely above a whisper. Her eyes rolled beneath their lids for a moment before she finally managed to open them. It seemed to take her a while to focus on Scarlett, but when she did she dragged a hand over one of hers. Scarlett eagerly took hold of it, intertwining their fingers so that Frances' hand couldn't slip away.

Scarlett could only watch her and cry. She had no words. All three of them were beyond mere sickness.

They were dying.

They were dying, and everyone in the house knew it.

"Frances, what can I do?" Scarlett eventually managed to ask, clinging to the question as much as she was clinging to the woman's hand. *Give me something to do. Anything. Tell me how to make things better.*

The woman smiled sadly, though it took effort to do so. "I have regretted it," she said slowly. "All this time, though I wouldn't admit it, I have regretted it."

"Regretted what?"

"Sending you away. Having you discover the truth. Hearing you call me Frances instead of mother. I regret it all."

"Don't say that," Scarlett immediately protested. "You were right to do it. I was in the way, I was –"

"You were not. You never were. I just couldn't see it. But, now..."

Frances coughed violently against her shoulder. When she finally stopped the fabric of her smock was spotted with blood.

"Look after your father when we're gone, Scarlett. You were always a good girl. I should have loved you better."

227

"You loved me just the way I needed, Mama," Scarlett whispered, wide-eyed and genuine even though the words were technically a lie. Hadn't she always longed for an ounce of warmth from her mother – for her to act with Scarlett the way she acted with Rudy and Elias? It seemed like such a hollow, worthless longing, now.

For her mother was dying and her tiny, helpless brothers were, too.

Eventually Scarlett tore herself away from the bed and pulled her father out of the room with her, down the stairs to his study.

Scarlett stared at him, whose face was even gaunter than her own. "Why didn't you tell me sooner?"

"We thought they'd get better," he said, his expression pained and regretful. "It didn't seem like much at first. A typical fever. But it only got worse, and nothing Otto or anyone else could do would stop it. Otto thought it was poison, but he cannot find any in their system. He doesn't know why I'm unaffected."

"Poison?" Scarlett couldn't dare believe someone would poison her family. The Dukes were well respected and liked within Rowan – they had no enemies, and certainly none who would target a man's wife and children over the head of the family, instead.

"If it's poison, it's one that Otto and the healers do not know of."

"What about Nana? She has –"

"Your grandmother would be no more help than the healers that we already brought to see them, my love," he interrupted, though not unkindly.

Scarlett thought of Adrian Wolfe, a man who might well know what was poisoning her family.

No, she decided bitterly, *the man I* thought *was Adrian might know. The real Adrian is a liar and a con-man. I wouldn't be able to trust a word he said.*

And even if she wanted to ask for his help, Adrian was long gone.

Scarlett bit back another sob. "Let me at least go back and get Nana. She might know something. She might –"

"Scarlett, please!" Her father stared at her pleadingly as his hands clenched into the side of his desk. "Don't make this harder on everyone than it already is. Otto doesn't think they have much longer than a day or two left. Let's not squander them looking for a cure that does not exist."

But Scarlett couldn't accept this. She wasn't ready to resign to the knowledge that her mother and brothers were doomed to die. Perhaps it was because she had only just become aware of their circumstances now, whereas her father had been dealing with it for days and days.

No matter the reason for it, Scarlett wasn't going to

sit and watch her family fade away. Giving her father one, final hug, she ran off from the study and through the side door.

"Scarlett, come back!" her father shouted out after her. But Scarlett couldn't turn back, for if she did she'd never leave. It was a feeling she understood well.

She had to keep going. She had to work out how to fix it.

And she'd start by asking her grandmother.

CHAPTER TWENTY-SIX

Adrian

Adrian hadn't had an opportunity to find Scarlett on the day before the full moon – his first day transforming. He had just two chances left.

He felt inordinately foolish, hiding behind the trees closest to Heidi Duke's home in the hopes of spying Scarlett return when he still had full use of his human body. Today, however, it seemed as if his luck may finally have turned. Her nefarious witch of a grandmother seemed to have retired to bed early; if Scarlett would only return in the next hour or so then

Adrian would have the best opportunity he'd had all week to explain himself...and to warn Scarlett of the poisons that were going to kill her family.

Adrian stayed stock still when his over-sensitive ears picked up the sounds of somebody travelling along the road through the woods. Though he was desperate to run out immediately, the years he'd spent stalking prey as a wolf taught him to stay exactly where he was until Scarlett appeared. He couldn't risk waking up her grandmother, after all.

It was only when he spied Scarlett's blood-red cloak – the weather had taken yet another cold turn – that Adrian dared to move a muscle. He stalked out to the edge of the trees where they met the road, not daring to make himself visible from the windows of Heidi's little house by stepping clear of the camouflage the branches afforded him.

If he was caught he was dead.

"Scarlett," was all Adrian said, so quiet that nobody but the woman mere feet away from him on the road could hear.

Scarlett whipped her head around to find the source of the voice, eyes narrowing in fury as they spotted Adrian. They were rimmed in red; clearly she had been crying.

"Go away, Mr Wolfe," she replied, though she had the sense to keep her voice quiet.

"Scarlett, please. You must listen to me."

"Oh, I *must?* I don't get a choice in the matter? So typical of you."

Adrian shook his head in frustration. After years of not truly caring about anyone but himself he was finding it next to impossible to frame his words in a context that did not include him.

He sighed. "Your brothers. Your step-mother. How are they?"

Scarlett seemed taken aback by the question. She sniffed slightly and rubbed at her eyes, further confirming that she'd just been crying. "Why do you care about them?"

"Does it seem like they've been poisoned but the doctor can't find anything wrong with them?"

"I – what? What do you mean by that, Mr Wolfe?"

"Scarlett, please. Get off the road." He gestured through the trees behind them, eyes darting over to her grandmother's house and back again. "We need to speak in private."

But Scarlett didn't like this idea. She took a step away from Adrian, towards the house. "Every word you've ever spoken to me has been a lie. Why should I trust you now?"

He felt like screaming, though Adrian knew he deserved Scarlett's mistrust. But he was running out of time; glancing up he saw that the sun had already fallen well below the tops of the trees. "Two minutes," he said. "Give me two minutes. Surely what I said about your family's sickness warrants two minutes?"

Scarlett seemed torn. She looked at her grandmother's house with a complicated expression, then at Adrian, then back again. But finally she relented and slowly followed Adrian through the trees. He took her to the small clearing where the silver birch tree that was Sam stood, simultaneously innocuous and sinister to his eye.

When he stopped walking Scarlett rounded on him, cloak whipping around her ankles as she did so. "Okay, Mr Wolfe. Explain yourself."

He had no time to waste.

He had to dive right in.

"Your grandmother is responsible for what's happening to your family. She's poisoning your step-mother and your brothers. I imagine you'd have a better idea as to why she's doing this than I would."

Scarlett's face was blank as she replied, "I don't believe you."

"I saw the dolls!" Adrian exclaimed, wringing his hands as he struggled to keep his voice down. He took half a step towards Scarlett, then, upon seeing her reaction, took a step back. "The straw dolls. Three of them. And I saw the poisons she was soaking them in. She's killing them slowly, so nobody thinks to consider it murder."

"What are you talking about? Dolls? Potions? What do you think my grandmother is – a witch?" Scarlett almost laughed the last question out. But upon seeing Adrian's dark, serious expression she reconsidered. "This has got to be a lie. I know my grandmother has some dangerous extracts and plants in her collection, but doesn't every healer? There's no reason to suspect her –"

"Scarlett, would I be saying *any* of this if I didn't have absolute proof of her wrong-doing? What reason would I otherwise have to pit you against your grandmother?"

"Oh, how about that ridiculous grudge you've had against her ever since she caught you trying to con her?" Scarlett bit out. She crossed her arms against her chest and turned away from Adrian. "The one that caused you to use me to get back at her. I'd say that would be reason enough to try and turn me against her. Just one last laugh for the clever Adrian Wolfe."

"Have you not even once considered why I hold that grudge, you impossibly ignorant little girl?!"

Adrian hadn't meant the words that came out of his mouth. He really hadn't. But at that exact moment the sun finally set and an unbearable pain began to crackle down his spine, ringing through every nerve and begging for him to scream.

Scarlett turned around to face him immediately, her expression full of fury and contempt. "How *dare* you.

How dare you say that to me, you –"

But her words caught in her throat as she watched Adrian struggle to stand. He staggered on the spot, eyes roving wildly for something to grab onto. Then he looked down at his clothes, remembering that he needed to remove them before he transformed lest he destroy them altogether.

He collapsed to the forest floor amongst a pile of dead leaves, fingers fumbling with the clasp of his cloak before struggling with the buttons of his waistcoat.

"Mr Wolfe, what are you doing? What's happening –"

"My boots!" he cried through gritted teeth. "My boots. Take them off. *Take them off!*"

The tone of his voice brooked no argument, and though Scarlett was still furious and disgusted by his insult she dropped to her knees and swiftly unlaced the man's boots, pulling them off as Adrian shirked out of his shirt.

"You want to know how I know Heidi Duke is a witch?" he muttered, sweat on the back of his neck turning icy cold in the air as his teeth clattered against one another. He forced his eyes on Scarlett, who looked terrified. "You want to know why I hold *a grudge?* All I wanted was for her to reverse what she'd done to me! Watch what your grandmother does to people who don't want to sell her soul-destroying curses and see whose side you're on, Miss Scarlett."

Adrian just barely pulled out of his leggings before his bones began to break. He covered his mouth with both hands to hold in a scream. Every second of pain was made all the more agonising knowing that the woman he'd impossibly come to love was watching him, naked and vulnerable and monstrous.

Scarlett didn't move; she was transfixed. Her mouth gaped open as if she meant to speak but no words came out. And yet Adrian could see her cheeks glistening with new tears as her eyes grew wider and wider.

He had never wanted Scarlett Duke to see him like this.

After what felt like an eternity the pain stopped. Adrian shuddered as he slowly picked himself up onto his new legs, the dead, dark leaves falling from his fur as he did so. He didn't dare move closer to Scarlett. All he did was stare.

"Knock, knock, Mr Wolf..." Scarlett breathed. The words were oddly appropriate, being the first ones she'd spoken to Adrian in this form. Gingerly she crept forward on her knees, reaching out a hand until her fingers brushed against Adrian's wet, black nose. "You were...you've been watching the whole time."

Scarlett said nothing for a while. Her chest heaved in panic, though, as if she were struggling not to pass out. Adrian pushed his muzzle against her hand, reminding her that she wasn't alone. And then she whipped her head around, looking for something.

Or someone.

"Adrian, where's Sam?" she asked, voice dripping with dread. "He's not – he isn't sick, is he? He saw what my grandmother was doing, didn't he?"

Adrian couldn't answer with words, of course. He whined softly, licked Scarlett's hand, then turned and walked over to the silver birch tree. He sat beneath it, waiting for Scarlett to understand what he meant.

She stumbled over to the tree numbly, staring at the ghostly white branches in disbelief as she traced her hands over the grain of the trunk. "No..." she whispered. "She didn't...Adrian, tell me she didn't do this!"

He merely whined again. Scarlett collapsed beside him, back against the birch tree as she tried desperately to stifle a sob.

"Nana is trying to kill them. She's going to murder Rudy and Elias and my mother for...me. She's doing this for *me*."

Scarlett looked down at herself, disgusted. She clawed at the fastening of her cloak and ripped it open, tossing the bleeding fabric onto the floor. She was breathing too heavily; her expression wild. If Adrian had been a man instead of a wolf he'd have wrapped his arms around her.

Instead, he crawled into Scarlett's lap and nuzzled his head against her shoulder, licking the edge of her jawline and whining until she finally looked at him again.

"I'm so sorry, Adrian," she said, very, very quietly. Her fingers found their way into his fur, holding him tightly as she buried her head into his ruff. "I'm sorry. I'm sorry. Please help me. Please –"

Adrian tilted his head and gently nibbled her ear, which was fairly difficult given that he was a wolf. But it was enough to shock Scarlett out of her crying, who pulled away in surprise as she reached up and touched her ear.

"That was a lot more painful than you were intending, I think," she said, almost laughing despite herself. "Or I would hope. I guess with you it could go either way. Are you telling me I need to calm down?"

Adrian didn't say anything, because he was a wolf. At this point even *he* was getting tired of thinking such sardonic things. *I guess I can see why one might find me insufferably full of myself,* he concluded, altogether rather bemused despite the dire situation both he and Scarlett were in.

Scarlett smiled sadly as she rubbed a hand against Adrian's muzzle. "It's fairly obvious what you're thinking, even as a wolf. 'I obviously can't speak like this, little miss,' or, 'What do you expect me to do in response to your question? I'm a wolf!', right?"

Adrian pulled his lips back in what he could only hope was the lupine equivalent of a smile. To his relief, Scarlett laughed. She ruffled his ears.

"I think I might like you better like this, Adrian," she joked, "though given the circumstances you're not much use in this form, are you?"

Adrian snarled slightly at the insult, since he couldn't respond with his usual sarcastic charm. Scarlett seemed to get the point, though, and swatted his nose in response.

"Mind your manners, Mr Wolfe."

Oh, wonderful, Adrian thought. *She's having far too much fun with this. I'll never live it down.*

For a while Scarlett said nothing more, content to embrace the wolf that was Adrian while she cast occasional, furtive glances at the birch tree that was Sam.

Eventually she asked, "Can we get him out of there?"

Adrian nodded his head as best he could. Relief washed over Scarlett's face.

"Alright. Alright. That's good. And...how long are you stuck like this?"

He pointed his nose up at the moon in the sky, fat and luminous and not at all threatening to the eye.

Scarlett laughed bitterly. "But of course. Controlled by the moon. What a cruel sense of humour Nana has, to turn you into a wolf and Sam into a birch tree." The words came out in the form of a choked sob, which Adrian could do nothing about. He simply rubbed his face against Scarlett as his tail swept to and fro across her legs.

After a while Scarlett calmed down. She no longer smelled of fear, allowing Adrian to once more pick up on the usual scents he associated with her: vanilla, saffron and sandalwood. But now she also smelled of wolf. He didn't know how to portray this to Scarlett – to warn her to wash his scent off her before her grandmother found out.

"Tomorrow, when you're human again, we'll stop her," Scarlett said as she gently pushed Adrian off her and got to her feet. He nuzzled against her leg, feeling to his very core that he did not want Scarlett going anywhere near her grandmother's house.

He knew she had to.

Letting out one final whine, Adrian looked up at Scarlett's sad yet determined face. He nudged her hand with his nose, allowing Scarlett to scratch it before turning to flee through the woods. He knew he'd have to return for his clothes before the sun rose but, for now, all he wanted to do was run, and run, and run.

For all he knew tomorrow would be the last day of his life, or he and Scarlett would stop her grandmother and his curse would be lifted. For better or worse this was likely Adrian's final evening as a wolf.

He was going to make it count.

CHAPTER TWENTY-SEVEN

Scarlett

She didn't know how she found the nerve to walk through the front door of her grandmother's house. The kitchen – once so comforting and full of joy – filled Scarlett with disgust. She looked at the table, with its stains and its marks and its indentations.

That's where she sat and orchestrated the death of my family. Which is supposed to be her *family.*

Scarlett didn't know why her grandmother had done it. She wanted to know. She wanted to know the precise reason that a mother would want her daughter-in-law and precious grandchildren murdered. But the fact Scarlett was unharmed filled her with a sick, horrible certainty that it had to do with herself.

That only made her feel worse.

Her grandmother had already retired for the evening, despite the fact it was reasonably early. Scarlett was both greatly relieved and incensed by this – relieved because it meant Scarlett didn't have to confront the old woman immediately; incensed because she didn't understand how anybody could sleep knowing that they were slowly, tortuously killing people. *Children.*

Scarlett had to force back a sob as she made her way through to her bedroom as quietly as possible. She was starving but her stomach was writhing like a thousand snakes. She'd never be able to keep any food down. In the morning she would eat. In the morning she'd get her strength back and confront her grandmother.

She was grateful she did not have to do it alone.

Adrian, Scarlett thought ruefully as she undressed. Part of her was still furious and confused with him, of course. He had admitted to using Scarlett as a means to get back at her grandmother. But – now that she knew *what* her grandmother had done to him – Scarlett quickly found her anger dissipating. Adrian had simply wanted his life back.

And he mentioned not wanting to give Nana a 'soul-

destroying curse'. Scarlett thought hard about everything else Adrian had said and done. How the first thing he had wanted Scarlett to do as soon as he saw her that day was to run. Clearly he had worked out her grandmother's horrific scheme then and there, which meant that...

"Saving me was more important than lifting his curse," Scarlett breathed out, her tiny, barely-uttered words swallowed by her pillow as she buried her face against it. And there had been no denying the way Adrian had looked at her – the fear, the desperation, the longing. Ultimately, in the end, Adrian had put Scarlett first.

Even if he took a typically twisted, Adrian Wolfe route to that decision. Scarlett wondered how he truly felt about her. What would the two of them be after they confronted her grandmother and, Lord help them, save her family? Could they repair what they had? Did Adrian even want that? Did Scarlett?

Tossing restlessly in bed she thought about Adrian, the wolf. He had been watching her for weeks. *Not just me,* Scarlett realised. *He was watching the house. He'd been keeping a close eye on what my grandmother was up to even as he crept up to my window and –*

Scarlett's face grew red and hot when she remembered discovering the wolf watching her dressed in nothing but her bed sheets. She had willingly let them fall. And if the wolf had been there from the moment Scarlett had taken off her robe...

"That pervert," she muttered despite herself,

somewhat outraged. It was no wonder Adrian had been so convinced that Scarlett would fall for him, though, if he had interactions with Scarlett as a wolf to base her thoughts and behaviour on. She had been completely different with the wolf than she had been with people – open and bold and honest. Adrian would have gleaned far more from those interactions than he ever did watching her in the marketplace of Rowan.

Scarlett glanced at her window. She wished Adrian was behind it, pawing at the glass and demanding her attention. Staring at her with those amber eyes that she had always deemed inhuman. Unbidden she thought back to when Adrian had unceremoniously kicked her out of his room in Mac's tavern. He had explained it away as a fit; a seizure.

Now Scarlett knew better.

Her heart hurt merely thinking about it. Adrian had been in so much pain, and all because of the whims of Heidi Duke.

Does he have to go through that every night? Scarlett wondered with concern. *He ran off when the sun set after Andreas interrupted us, too.* But Adrian had crept into her room and spent the night once, too. Sighing, Scarlett resolved to ask Adrian about the rules of his curse once he regained the ability to speak.

And then we'll deal with Nana. We'll deal with the woman who turns men into wolves and trees, and poisons little children because they have somehow

246

slighted her.

Scarlett didn't know how she fell asleep. All she knew was that she did and, when the darkness of unconsciousness fell over her, she dreamt. For the first time since her sixteenth birthday Scarlett dreamt of wolves and amber eyes and a woman who left a baby and ran away.

If not for that woman Scarlett's brothers and mother would be safe. For the woman who gave birth to Scarlett was not her mother and never had been.

She was merely a nightmare, haunting Scarlett with a life she could never have and never, she now realised, wanted.

*

"Red, dear, are you *ever* getting out of bed? It's almost midday!"

Scarlett forced herself awake with heavy, laboured blinks. She sat up in bed, rubbing at her eyes and wondering for a moment why her whole body felt raw and on edge.

And then everything hit her at once.

She dressed and stumbled through to the kitchen, smoothing flyaway hairs back as she sat down at the table. Forcing a smile on her face she grinned apologetically at her grandmother.

"Sorry, Nana. Clearly I needed to sleep."

Her grandmother came over and inspected Scarlett's face, turning her chin one way and then the other as she frowned. "Maybe you need some more. Why are your eyes red, Scarlett?"

Scarlett began to cry in earnest. She didn't even have to force it – merely thinking about her family, dying together at the hands of her grandmother was enough to warrant fresh tears.

The old woman hugged her fiercely; Scarlett struggled not to flinch. "Red, my love, whatever is wrong?"

"I-it's my mother, and Rudy and Elias. They're sick. They're dying. Did Papa say nothing to you about this?"

"This is the first I've heard of it," she replied as she pulled away. There was something odd about her expression when she added on, "But don't call that woman your mother, dear. I know it's easy to get sentimental hearing such news but you should still remember who and what she is."

Scarlett bristled. She had wanted to wait for Adrian to appear – indeed, she had to wonder where he was – but if her grandmother was going to say such things then Scarlett wasn't going to take the comments lying down.

"She *is* my mother," Scarlett bit back. "The woman who abandoned me on a doorstep is less than nothing to me. Frances raised me whichever way she could. I love her just as much as I love my father and my brothers."

Her grandmother was surprised by the retort. It took a little too long for her to fix her expression. "And what of your grandmother, Red?" she asked quietly. "Do you love Frances as much as your grandmother, who has always cared for you more than her? Who has always loved you more, and wanted what was best for you?"

"Nana –"

"They will die, Red. It's tragic, yes, but necessary. They were in your way. *Our* way."

Scarlett didn't dare believe her ears. Though she believed Adrian, it was a different thing entirely to hear her grandmother admitting to her crimes in such a cool, collected voice.

She feigned ignorance. "What do you mean, Nana? How are they in my way?"

Her grandmother's eyes flashed dangerously. "You really think I was going to let that woman get her way after kicking you out? Had she allowed you to stay in the main house as your father's heir then I wouldn't have touched her – or her little brats. Even after I was unceremoniously expelled from the house for supporting Richard's decision to keep you, I still would have left her alone." She paused, moving over to the open front door and closing it before pulling a curtain over the window. "You know, I never wanted Richard to marry Frances. It was your grandfather that insisted upon it. Forcing your father into a loveless marriage, just like I was. Of course, your grandfather didn't last long after that."

The horror of her words – the revelation that Scarlett never met her grandfather because his wife saw fit to get rid of him; the confirmation that Frances and Rudy and Elias' dire situation was because of Scarlett, and that her grandmother didn't seem to care about the evil consequences of her actions – caused Scarlett to stand up and back away towards the door.

But her grandmother merely smiled. "Where do you think you're going, Red? After your little rendezvous with Adrian Wolfe last night I don't think I can trust you to set foot outside these walls."

Scarlett gaped at her in disbelief. "How did you –"

"I really did treasure that cloak, Scarlett. Perhaps don't leave it out for the wolves next time."

Her grandmother pointed into a dark corner of the kitchen. For there lay the muddied, shredded ruins of the once beautiful red cloak Scarlett had, until yesterday, been fiercely enamoured with. Now it made her feel sick to look at it.

"You won't get away with this," Scarlett muttered, though there was neither strength nor conviction to her words.

Her grandmother merely laughed as she put on a dark cloak of her own. She picked up a basket which hung by the door, filled with three straw dolls dyed a sickly, discomfiting greenish purple colour.

She pointed at Scarlett. "This woman shall not set

250

foot outside this house. Until I return or should die let this spell hold true." Then she placed her hands upon the door and spoke to the house itself. "And do not let her out."

Scarlett shook with rage when she realised her grandmother had cast magic upon her. "You – you would put me under your control like this?"

"Just until your *mother* and her twins have sadly passed away. Now, I have a son to console and bring back under my wing. Wait and see, Scarlett; this will be good for you. With this you will have your previous reputation, fortune and opportunities back. We both will. Know that I love you, dearly."

With a swish of her cape her grandmother was gone, leaving Scarlett standing in the kitchen alone. She hadn't even been given a chance to confront her properly – about Adrian, about Sam, about anything.

Furiously she let out a scream. A long, outrageously loud and soul-rending scream. Scarlett had never made so much noise in all her life.

But it didn't matter.

Her grandmother was gone and she was locked away.

Scarlett had lost before she'd even had a chance to fight.

CHAPTER TWENTY-EIGHT

Adrian

When Adrian heard Scarlett's high pitched, blood-curdling scream he feared the worst.

Heidi cannot have harmed her, he thought with increasing panic. *She can't.*

It had taken Adrian much too long to fully recover from transforming back into a human. The process had been blindingly excruciating, and seemed to take even longer because of the urgency with which he needed his true form back. It was as if Heidi Duke's curse *knew* what was at stake and was working against Adrian, hindering him at every possible turn.

A few more transformations like that and I'll either die or not come back from my wolf form, he thought with chilling certainty. *If I don't die confronting the witch, anyway.*

Adrian spared barely a moment upon hearing Scarlett screaming, flinging on a shirt, leggings and boots before stocking up every secret pocket of his cloak and darting through the woods in the direction of Heidi's house. He wondered if the old woman would still be there...and what had happened to her grand-daughter.

"Let Scarlett be okay," Adrian muttered through his teeth as he rushed past tree after tree after tree, not daring to think she would truly be harmed. When finally the house became visible Adrian quickly checked on Sam Birch the tree, relieved to see that Heidi had left him that way instead of eliminating him as a precaution.

Once Adrian could be sure Scarlett was okay he'd set about saving Sam. They needed all the help they could get.

When he reached the front door Adrian was unsurprised to find that it wouldn't open. Steeling his nerves he kicked it with everything he had, which only left his body jarred with the force of the action. The door didn't budge.

He wasted no time in trying the kitchen window,

instead, but the glass seemed suspiciously unbreakable. Adrian rushed around to the back of the house to try Scarlett's window instead.

When he spied her wrenching out the drawers of her dressing table through the window he almost laughed with relief. Other than looking sleep-deprived and frenetic, Scarlett seemed fine.

Well, as fine as I could expect, given the situation, Adrian thought as he banged his fist against the glass to get Scarlett's attention.

Her face lit up when she saw him; it filled Adrian with an unbearable amount of love for the young woman in front of him.

"What happened to the house?" he shouted through the window, and then, "Where is your grandmother?"

Scarlett's face reverted to looking panicked. She rushed over to join Adrian at the window, holding up a hand against the glass as he instinctively did the same. To be so close and yet not touching was torment.

"She's gone. She trapped me. She put a spell on me!"

Adrian frowned. "Did she cast one on the house, too?"

"Yes! Adrian, what do I – what do we do?"

He smiled softly despite himself. He glanced behind Scarlett, noticing Jakob's silver snowdrop lying on the floor where Scarlett had unceremoniously thrown it aside in her haste to find something of use in her dressing table.

Scarlett followed his gaze with suspicion. She retreated from the window and picked up the beautiful, innocuous flower, returning with it clasped between both of her hands.

"Why were you looking at this, Adrian?"

His smile turned into a fiercely protective grin. "Because I enchanted it. The spell your grandmother cast on you will not work."

"You – when did you do that?"

"The night I crept into your room and eavesdropped on your conversation with Sam."

Scarlett seemed taken aback. "But that was before... you still meant to leave me. To use me. And you didn't know what my grandmother was up to."

Adrian laughed bitterly. "I didn't need to know what she was planning to know I wouldn't want you to ever fall prey to her magic, after what she did to me. And Scarlett, though it won't mean much, I truly am sorry for –"

"You don't have to be sorry," she interrupted, before shaking her head and adding, "No. Take that back. You do. Very sorry. So sorry you'll want to spend the rest of your life making it up to me."

He gave her a lop-sided grin at the foolish, wonderful

remark. "Do you mean that?"

"If you can help me save my family then I'm open to discussing it."

Adrian couldn't help but laugh. He never thought he and Scarlett would be able to repair their barely-begun relationship. Now, knowing that they could, he was determined more than ever to best Heidi Duke as quickly and as efficiently as possible.

To that end he forced himself back to the very real problem at hand. He stared at Scarlett seriously. "What *exactly* did your grandmother say to enchant the house? Do you remember?"

Scarlett frowned as she remembered. "She said, 'And do not let her out'."

"That was all?"

"I guess she thought the spell she'd put on *me* was more than sufficient."

"Good thing I'm an under-handed con-man, then," Adrian replied with a snort.

"We need to talk about that con-man thing after all of this is over."

"I imagine we do. But for now...it's exactly what we need."

Scarlett seemed taken aback. "What do you mean?"

"Head through to the kitchen and wait by the door."

"Adrian –"

"Just do it."

And so Scarlett dutifully did as she was told. Adrian jogged back around to the front door, too, and when he saw Scarlett through the window he knocked upon the door.

"Adrian, what are you doing?"

"I have come for dinner, or have you forgotten, Miss Scarlett? Won't you please let me in?"

"I – yes?"

"Don't say it as a question. Will you let me in?"

"Yes; please come in, Mr Wolfe."

"Okay, try opening the door."

To Scarlett – and, if he was being truthful, Adrian's – surprise, the door swung open. Adrian stepped over the threshold into the kitchen where a stunned Scarlett stood. He wasted no time in closing the gap between them and embracing her, his lips finding hers and bruising them with kisses as if his life depended on it.

He supposed it did.

Scarlett wound her fingers through his hair, desperately keeping Adrian as close as possible even though they both knew the moment couldn't last for ever.

Eventually it was Adrian who pulled away. "Where

did your grandmother put the spell on the house? Do you know where the straw dolls are?" he asked, more breathless than he had been after running all the way through the woods to the house.

It took Scarlett a moment or two to respond. Her eyes darted to the door, so Adrian closed it. "She took the dolls with her. As for the door, she placed her hands on it and said the spell," she explained. She narrowed her eyes. "How did you know you could open the door by asking if you could come in?"

Adrian scratched his chin. Then he riffled through some of his potions as he replied, "Just so long as you're not trying to get out, there's no reason for the door not to open. Now, to get you out, on the other hand..."

He let out a noise of satisfaction when he came across the vial he was looking for – it was pitch black and seemed to reflect no light whatsoever. When Adrian opened the bottle to pour some of the stuff on his fingers it seeped out like an ugly, poisonous sludge.

"What *is* that?" Scarlett asked curiously when Adrian smeared it into the grain of the wood.

"It blocks blocking spells and curses," Adrian explained. "I actually drink a little of it every day. It's disgusting."

"Why don't you just use that stuff you used on my snowdrop? So nothing will affect you?"

He gave her a side-long glance. "I have a bad curse

placed upon me already. It wouldn't work. It would be like an oxymoron; I'm already cursed so the spell believes itself to have failed. Magic is a tricky business. You should be able to leave now."

Scarlett gazed at Adrian with something he hadn't seen from her before – reverence. "You know so much," she murmured as Adrian opened the door and Scarlett, with some trepidation, walked outside.

Nothing stopped her.

She was free.

He smiled in satisfaction. "I *did* tell you I learned much from my parents. And after what happened with your grandmother I made it my business to know as much about magic as I possibly could."

"I figured you had probably lied about your past to get me to feel sorry for you," Scarlett admitted.

"A reasonable thought. But everything I told you about me was the truth."

"Apart from the fact you turn into a wolf."

He chuckled. "I guess you're right. I don't really know how I was supposed to slip that into casual conversation, though. Do you?"

"Not really, no." And then, when Adrian headed to the garden and picked up a large, wicked-looking axe, she asked, "What are you doing with that, Adrian?"

He grinned; eyes shining with some kind of mad amusement.

"I have some firewood to make."

CHAPTER TWENTY-NINE

Scarlett

"You don't mean – you can't chop Sam down, Adrian!" Scarlett cried out in horror.

Adrian merely laughed. "How else do you propose we get him out of the tree?"

"I thought he *was* the tree?"

He shrugged, hefting the axe over his shoulder as the two of them walked through the woods towards the telltale silvery branches of Sam-the-birch-tree. "It's a bit of both. Either way, this is how we free him."

"Don't you have a potion or spell or something that can get him out?"

A sly, wicked smirk twisted up the edge of his lips. "Maybe."

"So use it!"

"Why should I waste one of my expensive spells on Birch?"

"*Adrian!*"

He laughed when Scarlett whacked his arm. "I'm kidding, of course. I have no such spell or potion on me. I'm not too familiar with transfiguration magic, given how taboo it is. It's difficult – near impossible, even – to find any useful information on the subject. And trust me...I would know."

Scarlett was silent as she considered this. But she didn't like the idea of cutting down the birch tree; not one bit. "What if it doesn't work?" she asked nervously when Adrian took a few swings of the axe through the air, testing his aim.

"If it doesn't work then he'll be turned back into a human when the spell-caster dies. You can see our predicament; we could really use Sam's help *before* that happens."

"I – I hadn't thought about the fact that Nana – that she would have to..."

Adrian put down the axe in order stroke the side of Scarlett's face with a hand. He looked at her sadly. "There's no way this can end with her still alive. I'm so sorry, Scarlett."

She gazed at her feet. But then, when she finally looked back up at Adrian, her eyes were set and determined. She held a hand out.

"Give me the axe."

"Scarlett?"

"It's my fault Sam ever got so involved in this. I'll cut him down...and face whatever consequences that result from doing so."

Adrian stared at Scarlett with pride. She wondered why. With a grim smile he picked up the axe and handed it over to her; she staggered under the weight of it for a moment before grounding her feet and finding her balance.

"Where should I chop?" Scarlett asked, uncertain now that the axe was actually in her hands.

"As close to the bottom as possible, I'd wager."

"You'd *wager*?"

"Just swing the axe at the tree, Scarlett. I doubt you even need to chop the whole thing down."

Scarlett remained dubious but, with no other advice to follow, she took aim at the base of the birch tree, inhaled deeply, and swung.

The steel-headed axe bit deep into the tree. With a struggle Scarlett removed it, then hacked at the tree a second time. A third. A fourth.

"Have you ever considered a career as a woodcutter?" Adrian asked, somewhat impressed. For Scarlett's cuts were in almost exactly the same place; Adrian knew that, had he been the one swinging the axe, the cuts would have been haphazard.

She rolled her eyes. "Sam taught me how to do it properly."

"How fitting that you're chopping *him* down, then."

"When do you think it'll be enough?"

Adrian walked over and inspected the tree. It seemed fairly close to falling under its own weight.

"Give me the axe, Scarlett. I'll finish it off."

Since she was breathing heavily and her forehead was shining with sweat, Scarlett dutifully complied.

Adrian didn't even look to see where he was swinging before he threw all his weight behind one strike and hit the tree. It swayed dangerously for a few seconds and then, when Adrian gave it a kick, fell over.

There was an overwhelmingly bright pulse of silver light; Scarlett closed her eyes and held a hand up against it. When finally she could see again the tree was gone, replaced with a very startled-looking Sam spread haphazardly on the forest floor.

He leapt to his feet with a cry, eyes darting wildly from Adrian to Scarlett and back to Adrian again. "I was a tree. I was a *tree.* I –"

"You were a tree," Adrian echoed back somewhat unkindly. "We get it."

"How much do you remember, Sam?" Scarlett asked, running a comforting hand up and down Sam's arm as he struggled to wrap his head around what happened to him.

He shook his head. "I – everything? Sort of? I heard you talking to me a few times, Mr Wolfe. And I was aware of Scarlett's grandmother coming to pick up her cloak this morning – Scarlett, your grandmother!"

"She knows," Adrian said. "She knows everything. Speaking of which, perhaps this is a conversation best had on the road. Care to help us take the old witch down and save Scarlett's family, Sam?"

Sam glared at him as if the answer was obvious. "I've only ever wanted to help her. Unlike you."

"If you could both cooperate that would be *wonderful,*" Scarlett cut in, struggling to reign in her irritation at their petty rivalry even in the face of mortal danger.

Adrian smiled easily as they rushed off. "But of

course. I'm game if Birch is. After all, I could have left him as a tree."

"Why do you like this man, Miss Scarlett?!" Sam couldn't help but exclaim as he picked up the axe that lay forgotten on the ground before they rushed through the woods. All around the wolves were howling, even though it was the afternoon, but they knew Adrian's scent. They would not bother him after so long, even as a human. But they unnerved Sam and, to a much higher degree, Scarlett.

Adrian sidled up against Scarlett and brushed his lips against her ear, saying, "Don't worry. They're just talking to each other. They won't touch us. You're safe. Don't listen to the wolves."

Sam got his answer in that moment, in the quiet way Adrian reassured Scarlett and she immediately trusted him. He saw the way her face flushed having Adrian so close, and the change in her expression when she locked eyes with him, and he realised why Scarlett had been hit so hard when Adrian seemingly betrayed her.

She loved him, and she knew it. Sam never had a chance.

The townspeople of Rowan looked at the three of them curiously as they bolted along the streets, Adrian barely dressed and looking like he had spent the night in the forest (which he had), Sam ruddy-faced and carrying an axe over his shoulder, and Scarlett, who looked half a vengeful, beautiful phantom in her red dress and dark, unruly hair.

When finally they reached the Duke estate the grounds were eerily quiet. Scarlett glanced uncertainly at the men on either side of her.

"Do we...just go in through the front door?" Sam asked, a look of blank confusion on his face.

Adrian considered the ornate gates. "Let me walk through first. Just in case."

He stepped forward before Scarlett could stop him. When nothing happened, both Sam and Scarlett followed him with some relief. When they reached the front door, though, they were surprised when it swung open to reveal Scarlett's father.

"Papa!" she cried out when she saw him. "Papa, where's my grandmother? She –"

"Who are these fellows, my love?" he interrupted. There was something not quite right about his expression. It was glassy and unnerving and set Scarlett immediately on edge.

"That's not important, Papa," she pressed on. "We need to get into the house and –"

"Oh, that won't be necessary. I think you should stay out here for the time being. I wouldn't want you to have to see your brothers. They're so sick."

Scarlett stared at her father, dumbfounded. She turned to Adrian, whose expression was pained.

"He's been enchanted. He's –"

But Adrian's next words were caught in his throat when he spasmed and collapsed to the floor. He cried out in pain and, when his spine began to snap and bend, Scarlett realised with horror what was happening.

"But the sun hasn't set! Why is this –"

"It was a mistake for you to try to come here, Mister Wolfe."

Scarlett's eyes darted back to the doorway, where her grandmother now stood beside her father. She was smiling an ugly smile that twisted her old, weathered features into something monstrous.

She stared at them all in disbelief. "You really think I wouldn't have set up counter-measures against the one man who could stop me? Especially since, it seems, he was able to undo my spells on the two of you," she added on, inclining her head towards Sam and Scarlett.

"But never mind," she continued on airily, as if Adrian wasn't howling in pain on the gravelled path as Sam stared on in horror and Scarlett bent down to try and fruitlessly help. "Red, dear, why don't you and Samuel come on in where I can keep watch over you? And as for our dear friend Mister Wolfe..."

Adrian had finally finished transforming. He stood there, trembling on four legs whilst he whined and shook his great, furred head. Scarlett thought that he still looked very much like he was in agony.

It was nothing compared to the look in his eyes at what happened next.

Heidi Duke snapped her fingers, and the grounds went up in flames.

For half a second Scarlett saw Adrian's pupils contract in his beautiful, amber eyes, full of sheer terror and animalistic panic that he couldn't push away.

He fled.

CHAPTER THIRTY

Adrian

He hadn't wanted to run. He'd wanted to stay and rip out Heidi Duke's damnable throat, freeing him from his curse once and for all. He'd wanted to save Scarlett's family.

Now he could do none of those things.

I didn't even tell Scarlett what to do with the straw dolls, Adrian realised mournfully as he continued to flee full-pelt out of the Rowan estate. *Just take a hint from the fire, Scarlett. Burn them, burn them, burn them.*

Adrian didn't stop running until he reached a stream that ran along the back of Scarlett's family estate. He'd had the sense not to run in the direction of the rest of Rowan, where in all likelihood Adrian would be shot on sight. He was a wolf, after all, and that's what people were trained to do if they saw a creature such as him prowling along the streets.

I hate myself, he thought as he finally stopped, panting and deliriously terrified even now, away from the flames. He lapped at the cold, clean water of the stream, revelling in how it slowly brought him back to his senses. *I hate being a wolf. I hate being a slave to my instincts.*

If he were human he would have laughed bitterly at the irony of that statement. For hadn't he *always* been a slave to his instincts, from the moment both of his parents were stripped away from him? Adrian had looked out for nobody but himself, only doing what served his best interests or amused him. He hadn't done anything that went against his instincts – that helped someone else.

Until I truly got to know Scarlett. Until I fell in love with her. With a panging sense of regret Adrian realised that he hadn't yet told Scarlett his true feelings. *And now I may never get another chance.*

He looked back at the Rowan property, the grounds still very much alight with brutal, dancing flames. Adrian couldn't go near them. He *couldn't.*

He had to.

If Heidi Duke and her ensorcelled son were keeping a close eye on Scarlett and Sam then that meant they couldn't look for the poisoned straw dolls Scarlett said her grandmother had taken with her.

Not to mentioned the torn remains of Adrian's cloak – and the spells and potions that were hidden in the pockets – likely still lay where he had transformed. Even if the cloak burned to nothing everything stored within it would be safe, since Adrian protected anything of value in his possessions against fire and water. He could only hope that Heidi hadn't taken the cloak inside with her.

It means I have to go through the fire, Adrian thought despairingly. But Scarlett was relying on him doing so. Her happiness depended on it.

Which meant Adrian's did, too. It was an odd sensation; one which he had not felt stir his heart for a long, long time.

And so Adrian rolled himself in the stream, drenching his outer coat in freezing water until it began to soak through to his thick, fluffy inner coat. Whining despite his resolve, and with his tail firmly between his legs, Adrian darted back towards the hellscape of the flaming Duke grounds before his animal instincts could force him against it.

The flames were licking up the sides of trees and bushes of all shapes and sizes; the grass turned to straw and then ash as fire razed it back to the very soil it sprouted from. Only the gravelled paths throughout the grounds remained unburned, but the air was hot and poisonous with choking, suffocating smoke. Adrian resisted breathing in as much as possible as he flinched from the heat, scrabbling across the gravel back towards the front of the house.

He spied his cloak where he had abandoned it – the fire had not yet reached it. And so Adrian bolted over and grabbed it between his teeth, pulling it along the path until he reached what looked like a side door into the Duke residence. Without hands to unstopper bottles and a human voice to utter spells everything inside was useless to him...but it wouldn't be to Sam or Scarlett. All he had to do was find the *right* magic for them to use.

With a grin that was literally *wolfish* Adrian thought of the axe Sam had prudently brought along. He located the potion he'd used to get through the spell Heidi had put on her front door and held it gently in his mouth. If he could pour the putrid, black liquid over the edge of the blade then Sam would be able to use the axe to cut the witch down.

It was the only potion with a chance in hell of working. It was their best shot.

Adrian had to get inside the house first.

Peeking in through the glass panel in the door he saw that nobody was in the corridor. Standing up on his hind legs Adrian pushed down on the handsomely carved door handle until it finally gave way, then nosed the door open inch by inch until he just barely managed to

273

squeeze through.

To think I'd ever have to waste five minutes trying to open a door, he bemoaned. Adrian never thought he'd explicitly miss having opposable thumbs, but with every passing moment spent as a wolf when he *needed* to be a man he decided never to take for granted the body he had been born with ever again.

If I survive, that is.

The first room he passed on his left was what appeared to be a study. The door was ajar, and the room was empty, so Adrian crept in to investigate. And there, sitting innocuously in a wicker basket, were the three straw dolls he had seen Heidi make, seeped in poison. Even with his limited colour perception Adrian could tell that the dolls were close to saturation, which meant Scarlett's family had perhaps hours left to live, if not minutes.

They might even been dead already.

But Adrian could not think like that. Carefully juggling the vial of blocking potion and the handle of the wicker basket in his mouth, he retreated from the study with the full intention of going back outside and flinging the wretched dolls into the fiery wreckage of the Duke grounds.

"What is a wolf doing in my study?"

Adrian flinched at the voice; it was Richard Duke, eyes glassy and expression lifeless like a human-sized doll. Had his mouth not been full he would have snarled at the man and snapped his teeth until he got past, but the things held by Adrian's jaws were too precious to let go of.

He tried to barge his way through the door but the man, unnervingly quickly, grabbed a poker from the nearby, empty fireplace and speared it straight through Adrian's right flank.

Thoughts of keeping hold of the straw dolls and the black potion were all but lost as Adrian yowled in pain. He struggled back onto his feet, though his right leg wouldn't take his weight, as Richard pulled out the poker with the intention of striking again.

"*Adrian!*"

Scarlett bolted towards him and pushed him free of her father, who struck the wall instead. She was followed by her grandmother who looked furiously confused.

"Why won't any of my magic work on you, Red?" She glared at Adrian. "What have you done to her, wolf?"

Adrian could do nothing but growl half-heartedly. Scarlett stroked his bleeding, matted fur even as he whimpered, her eyes full of horror at the blood pouring out of his wound. But he nudged her hand with his nose, urging Scarlett to pay attention to the dolls. She could deal with him later.

It took her a second to understand what Adrian was

meaning as he glanced from the dolls to the door, where the fire could be seen roaring away through the glass. But then she nodded, grabbed the dolls and made for the door, slamming it open just as her grandmother screamed out.

"Stop her, Richard!" Heidi called out, making her way down the corridor to pull out the poker from the wall as her son chased after his only daughter. She glared at Adrian. "It's time I finish you off, Adrian Wolfe."

But then there was a *whoosh* of air behind her and Heidi only just ducked out of the way of Sam, swinging his axe so powerfully it smashed the wooden panelling of the wall when the blade connected with it.

"I should have burned you to the ground when you were a tree," Heidi glowered, carefully avoiding the man as she took a few steps back towards Adrian. "But it's no matter; Frances and the boys are breathing their final breaths. Even if my dear Scarlett burns the dolls it will be too late."

The grin on Heidi's face was more inhuman than any Adrian – even as a wolf – had ever smiled. When Sam swung his axe at the old woman once more he was shocked and appalled when it deflected off her, as if Heidi was made of steel instead of flesh.

She laughed maliciously. "You can't kill me so easily, Samuel. Now you, on the other hand..." She flung the poker at Sam with surprising strength and accuracy, slicing straight through the side of the arm he held the axe with. Sam let out a roar of pain as he dropped the weapon, clutching at the wound and staring at Adrian as if he must surely know what to do next.

But Adrian didn't. They were both injured, and Heidi was protected. Outside he could hear Scarlett shouting and protesting against her father. Every second spent fighting instead of helping Frances, Rudy and Elias only sent them further to their graves.

But then Adrian spotted the cracked vial of black potion slowly dripping into the carpet, and he acted without thinking. He lunged for it, breaking the glass open with sharp teeth until the inside of his mouth was coated with the disgusting liquid. Resisting the urge to heave and spit it out he skittered across the floor and crunched his jaws around Heidi's leg and, when she screamed, let her go and licked the axe, covering it in the same black potion that was also seeping into the puncture wounds on the witch's leg.

He shared the briefest of glances with Sam, who wasted no time in picking up the axe and struggling with it left-handed.

Just one hit, straight and true, Adrian begged, cowering into the corner when Heidi locked eyes with him and began to utter the beginning of a curse that he did not like the sound of at all.

But Sam's swing missed, and Heidi limped forward as if she didn't consider him a threat at all. She continued weaving her spell, and Adrian's heart suddenly felt like it

277

was being crushed. He couldn't breathe. He couldn't see.

This is how I die, he thought deliriously. *In vain. Only fitting for a vain man.*

"Good-bye, Mr Wolfe," Heidi said with cruel satisfaction. "May you never –"

But her next words were cut off.

As was her head.

With one fell swoop Sam's axe found its mark and, with it, destroyed the vice-like grip the witch had on Adrian's heart.

As well as the hold she had on his soul.

"You're not so useless after all, Birch," Adrian muttered as he transformed back into a human faster than he'd ever transformed before, though he could barely stay conscious let alone speak. Sam didn't look at him, instead staring blankly at the headless, bloody corpse of the woman who'd once been his employer.

Heidi Duke was gone.

Adrian had nearly died for it, but he was free and he was, miraculously, still alive.

He only hoped the same could be said for Scarlett's family.

CHAPTER THIRTY-ONE

Scarlett

The realisation that her grandmother must have died was immediate. Her father let go of her arms, which he'd twisted painfully behind her back in his accursed attempt to stop her from burning the straw dolls that were killing their family.

Scarlett had no time to spare to see if her father was alright, or if he knew what was going on. She immediately picked up the basket of dolls where they had fallen on the gravelled path and flung them into the fire surrounding them, watching them smoulder a sickening green until the flames, finally, engulfed them.

And it was just in time; the unnatural fire receded into nothing a mere minute later, the power that had lit it in the first place now completely spent. Scarlett stared out at the destruction it had caused with numb, shell-shocked eyes – everything was all black and ash and ugly curls of smoke still hanging in the air. She spared a thought for the town of Rowan, thankful that the flames had not left the confines of the Duke estate.

"Scarlett? Scarlett!" her father called out, reaching for her desperately as understanding and intelligence finally returned to his face. He was panicked; horrified. "What have I done? What has *she* done?"

"We have no time, Papa!" Scarlett exclaimed as she grabbed his hand and dragged him back inside.

She retched at the horror lain out before her eyes once she set foot through the door. For there stood Sam, clutching at a deep gash on his arm even as his fingers, slippery with blood, dropped his axe to the floor. Adrian lay against the wall with his eyes closed, once more human and completely naked but for the thick layer of blood covering much of his skin. His leg was still bleeding badly; his teeth covered in black, oozing liquid that he spat out onto the carpet without opening his eyes.

And then there was Scarlett's grandmother, headless. Lifeless. Dead.

"S-Sam," Scarlett stuttered. "Adrian –"

"My cloak," Adrian coughed and spluttered, just barely managing to gesture back behind Scarlett. "And my...clothes, if they're not burned to a crisp."

Blindly Scarlett complied, locating Adrian's cloak by the door. His clothes, however, were in ruins. When she returned she glanced at her father, who was struggling to comprehend the scene in front of him.

"Can you get him...something to wear?" she asked. "Anything."

Adrian waved her over as her father nodded, then rushed into the servant's quarters before returning with a plain, cotton shirt and a pair of leggings. Weakly Adrian took the cloak, and the clothes, and struggled into the shirt before searching through his cloak. When he located a jar the colour of pale jade he opened it with trembling hands, ran his finger inside the jar to collect a small amount of similarly coloured salve and spread it across the wound in his leg.

He sighed in plain relief before flinging the jar at Sam, who caught it clumsily in his left hand. "That'll stop the bleeding and encourage the healing process, witch-killer," he mumbled. Adrian pulled on the leggings Scarlett's father gave him with some effort, wincing and biting down on his lower lip in pain when the material grazed his wound.

Scarlett moved forward immediately to kneel by his side when Adrian tried to stand up. "Stay where you are, Adrian! You can't move, you've lost too much –"

"Your wife," Adrian cut in, staring at her father. "Your sons. Where are they?"

The man glanced upstairs. "In the master bedroom."

"Show me." And then, directed at Sam, "Go get cold, clean water and hot tea. Tell the kitchen staff to prepare clear broth and bread."

Sam didn't baulk at the commands. He merely nodded and rushed off to dutifully comply.

When Adrian tried and failed to stand on his own Scarlett took his arm and slung it over her shoulder. She took Adrian's cloak and crumpled it beneath her other arm. "Do you really think you can save them?" she whispered, not daring to hope.

"If they aren't dead already," he said, too exhausted to blunt his words. But it was the closest suggestion to a cure that both Scarlett and her father had heard so far, so the two of them exchanged a barely hopeful glance as he took Adrian's other arm and helped his daughter haul the man up the stairs.

"You look awful, by the way," Scarlett said when they reached the upstairs corridor. "Your clothes are soaked with blood already. You look like you bathed in the stuff."

"I must really love you, then, Miss Scarlett, to have ended up this way."

Scarlett said nothing. To hear Adrian confess *now,* of

all moments, was shocking and inappropriate and so glaringly Adrian Wolfe than she couldn't help but choke back a laugh.

"I love you too, you arrogant, narcissistic, no-good con-man."

Her father raised an eyebrow as they reached the door to the main bedroom. "That's the worst endorsement I could possibly hear as a father."

"I could have said a whole lot worse."

Adrian snorted. "Charming."

He was gently placed down on a chair by the bed; Frances, Rudy and Elias weren't moving. For a moment Scarlett felt like her lungs had been filled with water. She couldn't breathe. Her vision went blurry. And then –

"Still alive," Adrian murmured, having checked their pulses. "Still alive and better than I could have hoped. Scarlett, my cloak?"

She passed it over with numb fingers, then watched in astonishment as Adrian carefully riffled through the pockets and folds of the fabric until he located everything he needed. Scarlett would never have been able to identify even a single thing in Adrian's possession, yet there he sat nimbly mixing one vial of blue liquid into another as clear as diamonds before pouring in what looked to her eyes like sand and shaking the bottle vigorously.

When he was done the resulting solution was a brilliant turquoise, and as viscous as the black potion Adrian had used earlier on that day.

"Scarlett, help me out here," Adrian said, too focused on his work to look up at her. When she sat by his side he smeared some of the salve he'd created on her fingers. "Up their noses and on the roof of their mouth. Can you do that?"

Scarlett nodded before rushing to comply, just as Sam entered the room.

Adrian waved him over. "Excellent timing. Mix this into the water," he ordered, handing him over a sachet of powder.

"What's in there?" Scarlett's father asked, too curious to keep quiet any longer. "What's in the salve?"

"This and that," Adrian replied, sounding as sketchy and irreverent as ever. "They never really had any poison in their system, but it'll take a few hours for their bodies to fully register that. Their bodies are very weak; they're lacking the nutrients to recover properly." He glanced at Scarlett's father, who didn't like the sound of anything Adrian said at all.

He smiled slightly. "The salve will speed up the process of getting rid of the phantom poison's effects. The powder in the water is to help recover their strength, as well as to keep any pain at bay. When they're awake you must keep them all well hydrated and fed every two hours or so."

"So they're....my family is going to be –"

"They'll be fine. In a few days. Keep them all in bed for a week just to be sure, though."

Scarlett had never seen her father look at anyone the way he looked at Adrian. It was more than sheer gratitude – the man had saved his entire family. He needn't have, and he nearly died doing it, but he did it anyway.

When she was finished applying the salve and saw her brothers immediately begin to stir and their breathing ease up Scarlett let out a cry. She darted out a hand to hold her mother's when the woman's eyes slowly, laboriously began to open.

"Scarlett?" she coughed. Sam rushed over with a cup of water, clumsily holding it to her mother's mouth as she dutifully drank. When Sam moved away she smiled at her husband, who sat on the bed and stroked back her hair. "Richard, why are you all covered in blood? And who are these two young men?"

Adrian laughed, seemingly amused by the prospect of being referred to as young.

Scarlett resisted the urge to hit him across the head. "Mama, this is Adrian Wolfe, and this is Sam Birch." She reached out a hand to bring him back over. "They saved your life. They saved all of us."

Her mother beamed, and it lit up her gaunt, exhausted face. "Then it seems I owe you both a great debt of gratitude. Though perhaps we might wait a few days before talking through what happened."

"Absolutely!" Scarlett's father exclaimed. He looked at his daughter, then Adrian. "Scarlett, my love, perhaps you should see to Mr Wolfe's injuries downstairs. And – Sam Birch, was it?"

Sam nodded.

"Might I trouble you to keep helping me, just until I can have a servant bring Otto Sommer to the house?"

He nodded once more. "Anything I can do to help. It's all I've ever wanted."

Scarlett was overcome with affection for the man. She took his hands in hers, reached up and kissed him, very gently. "Thank you, Sam. I don't know what I could ever do to repay your kindness."

He blushed furiously, running a hand through his blonde hair gone ruddy with dried blood. "Don't let Mr Wolfe get away with any more of his tricks and I'll call it even."

"Hah!" Adrian bit out. "As if she could ever do that."

Scarlett ushered him out of the room before Sam, glaring, could fire back a retort.

"You could stand to act a little more mature, all things considered," she complained as she helped Adrian down to a room where the staff stored medical supplies. She ignored the lifeless body of her grandmother. She had to. "That was my entire family in a room, you know."

"As if you could really expect me to be anyone other than me," he said, easing himself into a chair as Scarlett found a rag and began cleaning his face.

She smiled despite herself. "I suppose not."

"You already told your father I was an arrogant, narcissistic con-man, anyway."

"You missed out no-good."

"An important omission, I realise."

"Do you really love me?"

Scarlett stared at Adrian, her blue eyes suddenly full of uncertainty and doubt. Adrian may have simply said he loved her because of the adrenaline running in his system, revelling in the sheer feeling of being alive.

But his amber eyes held none of the doubts Scarlett's did. They were clear and intent.

"Scarlett," he began, running a hand through her hair to urge her closer, until their noses were almost touching. "I have lied to you. Betrayed you. Teased you. Mocked you. But my love for you is the one thing that's remained true throughout everything, no matter how despicable my actions were. I love you. I love you. And if you really could find it in you to accept a wretched, barely human waste of a man as a companion –"

"Shut up, Adrian."

"You won't even let me finish my confession?"

Scarlett rolled her eyes. "You already said the important part. I won't let you wallow in self-serving deprecation. Because what kind of woman would I be if I let the man I love do that in front of my very eyes?"

Adrian's face lit up. He smiled a smile full of sharp teeth and genuine, overwhelming joy.

"Won't you kiss me, Miss Scarlett?"

Her lips brushed his – a promise of many more kisses to come.

"As if you had to ask, Mr Wolfe."

EPILOGUE

Adrian

When Scarlett demanded Adrian take her away from Rowan and teach her everything he knew – about magic, about healing, about the world – Adrian had been shocked but only too happy to oblige.

He got Scarlett Duke all to himself.

It was a dream come true.

Almost a year had passed since Adrian, Sam and Scarlett had taken down her grandmother and saved the rest of her family. Once Scarlett was sure her mother and brothers would recover, the two of them had set off to explore other lands together, Adrian working as a merchant whilst Scarlett studied and studied and then studied some more. They had not been back to Rowan.

Now they were.

He watched fondly as Scarlett's screaming, delighted, identical brothers ran into her arms, bowling her over until she fell to the dusty ground. Behind them stood Richard and Frances Duke, smiling and laughing as Scarlett struggled back to her feet.

Samuel Birch was there, too. When Richard Duke had asked the man what he wanted in return for saving the family he had asked, unexpectedly, to learn. As the miller's son he'd had little opportunity to educate himself past basic letters and numbers. He wanted more for himself than the life he'd been born to inherit.

Adrian couldn't help but respect the man, though when they caught each other's eyes they both glared.

"Uncle Adrian!" Rudy – he thought it was Rudy – called out. Adrian didn't know when the boys had begun referring to him as such, since he and Scarlett had been gone all year, but he had a sneaking suspicion it had something to do with the exotic gifts he sent back for the two of them on a regular basis.

He grinned at them. "You're both so tall now. It won't be long until you outgrow your sister."

They both beamed proudly at the idea; Scarlett

chuckled as she mussed up their hair.

"You have to keep eating your vegetables if you want to be taller than me."

"How was the journey home?" Richard asked, kissing his daughter on the cheek before shaking Adrian's hand.

"Horrible," Scarlett complained, making a face. "The sea was awful. So stormy – I honestly thought we were going to die more than once."

"Don't be so dramatic, Red," Adrian said. "It wasn't that bad. You just don't like travelling by boat."

"Touché."

Adrian glanced at Frances, before searching through his belongings and taking out a wooden box. He handed it over to her; inside was an ornate glass bottle filled with a liquid the colour of Adrian's eyes.

"I have it on good authority that your grandfather used to gift you this. Scarlett told me her father could no longer procure it, so I...took the liberty of sourcing it. There are a few more bottles in my luggage."

Frances opened the bottle, closing her eyes and sighing in contentment when she breathed in the scent. It filled Adrian's nose, too, which would forever be over-sensitive. Vanilla. Saffron. Sandalwood. Scents he was hopelessly in love with.

Frances enveloped Adrian in an embrace so tight he

almost winced.

"Thank you, Adrian," she exclaimed happily. When she pulled away she looked at her husband. "And you had your doubts he'd treat our daughter well. The man's a charmer through and through, Richard."

"Precisely the problem," both Richard and Sam grumbled.

Adrian could only laugh as Scarlett glowered.

"It's not for any of you to decide if Adrian is good for me or not," she complained.

"Oh, certainly not," her father chuckled. "I doubt anyone would dare cross you now, daughter."

She frowned. "What do you mean?"

"He means you look powerful," Adrian explained for him. "Intimidating. It's a good look on you."

"Sister isn't scary!" Elias – or perhaps Rudy – bit out. "She's exactly the same!"

"You'll understand why she's different when you're older, boys," Frances said mildly. Adrian had to wonder if she would ever tell her sons what had really happened to them. Part of him wanted them to know – to know what their sister had done for them.

But a bigger part of him wanted them to remain forever ignorant. Scarlett would never want them to know, after all.

"You seem to have learned much on your travels, going by your letters," Sam said to Scarlett.

She smiled broadly, glancing at Adrian. "There's so much to know, Sam. And Adrian is a wonderful teacher."

He brushed his hand against Scarlett's at the remark, informing her that he took her words to mean something far filthier than her original intention. The tips of Scarlett's ears grew red, and Adrian was very suddenly reminded of the fact they had not rested, in a real bed, for days.

And so Adrian turned to Scarlett's parents with an apologetic smile. "The two of us are admittedly very tired from our journey. I hope you won't take offence if we rest for a while."

Frances nodded in understanding. "You're welcome to stay in the house, of course, but I took the liberty of having your grandmother's house prepared for you, Scarlett."

There was barely an edge to her voice as she mentioned Heidi Duke. For the sake of her sons – and her husband, and Scarlett – Frances was careful about how she talked about the old woman.

Adrian glanced at Scarlett out of the corner of his eye, wondering what she would do.

She smiled sadly. "Thank you, Frances. We'll head to Nana's house, if that's okay."

"It's yours whenever you're ready to come home permanently, my love," Richard said. "Though if you'd rather a new house was built better befitting your name then of course –"

"No," she interrupted. "I'll take her house. I love it. I always have."

And so Adrian and Scarlett headed for the woods with a final wave at her family and Sam, who once more glared thunderously at Adrian.

"You think he'll ever like me?" he asked as they wandered beneath the boughs of the trees, content not to walk too quickly.

"Do you think *you'll* ever like him?"

"I never disliked him. I merely enjoyed irritating the life out of him."

"You're a terrible person."

"I'm aware."

In stark contrast to the year before, the late April weather was pleasantly warm. The air positively teemed with life; songbirds, frogs and foxes could be heard calling to each other.

But no wolves.

"When's the next full moon, Adrian?" Scarlett asked nonchalantly.

"Twelve days," he replied immediately before

grimacing when she laughed.

"Do you think you'll ever get that habit out of your system? Of knowing exactly when it is?"

"*You* spend almost seven years as a wolf every full moon then tell me if you're likely to forget when the next one is."

Scarlett squeezed his hand in response, dragging him along the path through the forest more and more insistently with every passing minute.

"What's the rush, little miss?"

She stared at him pointedly. "I can't be the only one longing for a bed."

"I'm longing for something *to do* in a bed...or, rather, someone."

Scarlett didn't even blush at the comment. Rather, she glanced behind Adrian before raising an eyebrow, lips full of mischief as they curled into a smile.

"Must it be a bed?" she asked coyly. Scarlett began to unlace the front of her dress tantalisingly slowly, safely tucking away the silver snowdrop she now habitually kept on her person when the sleeves of the white blouse she was wearing beneath her dress slipped from her shoulders.

Adrian could hardly contain his excitement at Scarlett's sudden boldness. Without another word he picked her up, Scarlett wrapping her legs around his waist as their mouths found each other and Adrian walked them off the road and in amongst the trees.

When he reached a clearing where the ground was covered in thick, spongy moss, Adrian fell upon it with Scarlett in tow. Her fervent hands wasted no time in unclasping his braces and unbuttoning his trousers, even as his hands slid up her thighs beneath her dress and urged her closer.

It didn't take long before Adrian was inside her, Scarlett sitting in his lap and gasping as the pair of them rocked together, breathless and desperate for each other.

"What would your parents think, seeing you so bold and debauched?" Adrian murmured against her ear. "And in a forest, no less. Unthinkable."

"It's a good thing they will never know, otherwise they'd kill the man responsible for making me this way."

He laughed as he planted kisses down her neck. "I don't think anyone was responsible for making you this way except you, Scarlett."

Scarlett's hands found Adrian's face and turned his lips back to her own, kissing him as if it were the first and final time they might ever do so. They didn't speak again for a long, long time.

Finally, when the sun was well below the line of the trees they pulled apart from each other. They lay on the forest floor, hands and knees and hems of clothes stained green whilst their chests heaved and their faces slowly lost their flush.

Scarlett turned her head and stared at Adrian until he stared right back. Her luminous eyes glittered in the low light of the forest. Scarlett had always loved Adrian's eyes; she would never know how deeply he loved hers.

"Promise me something, Mister Wolfe," she finally murmured.

He smirked at the name. "Anything, little miss."

"Never marry me."

"Only if you never marry me, either," Adrian laughed, pulling Scarlett against his chest and burying his face in her hair. It smelled of everything important to him.

It smelled of home.

And, most of all, it smelled of Scarlett Duke.

EXTRA CHAPTER

Scarlett

"I'm so thirsty I could drink an entire flagon of water!"

"How about wine, instead?"

Scarlett laughed good-naturedly. "I suppose we've been travelling for a while now. It wouldn't hurt to stop here for the night and enjoy ourselves."

All around them were the signs of a midsummer festival in full swing. Lanterns were strung from poles and ropes and shop fronts, casting the small town in a warm, amber glow. The dusk air was filled with spicy, sweet and savoury smells that caused Scarlett's mouth to water and her nose to twitch, desperate to follow them to their source. The cobbled streets were laden with merchants selling everything from food to fireworks to mysterious items whose purpose Scarlett could not identify.

One stall was selling nightingales enclosed in ornate, golden cages, which several children were admiring with wide and covetous eyes. The birds sang out from the prisons, adding their wonderful voices to the cacophony of sound bombarding Scarlett's ears. She felt an aching sadness for them, and longed to set them free.

"I should have brought all my stuff with me," Adrian mused as he wound his way through the throng. Scarlett could see him sizing up groups of women who looked likely to fall for his charms – those who would eagerly spend all their money on his largely useless spells.

"Good thing we're not here on business, then," she said, before sliding her hand behind Adrian's neck and pulling his mouth down to hers. *Those women can keep their eyes to themselves,* Scarlett thought, when Adrian wrapped his arms around her waist and held her close. He enthusiastically reciprocated her kiss; even after two years their desire for each other hadn't once wavered.

When they parted Adrian was smirking. He glanced at the closest group of young women, who were noticeably disappointed. "Jealous, Scarlett?"

"Oh, never, but I don't much relish the idea of

spending all evening watching every young and pretty thing falling at your feet."

"I could say much the same thing about you!" Adrian complained, "Though you seem to attract just about *every* man, not just the young and pretty ones."

Scarlett rolled her eyes, looped an arm through his and pulled the two of them down the street towards a well lit stall. It was true that she'd caught the attention of several men, but one look at Adrian was all they needed to know that they didn't stand a chance. For who could truly match a man such as Adrian Wolfe?

His head would grow three times as large as it is now if he knew I thought of him like that, Scarlett mused as she handed over several coins to the vendor in exchange for two large cups of spicy, dark-coloured wine. She relished the warmth of the liquid as it passed her lips and glided down her throat.

"This is truly excellent," she said, happily taking a larger gulp of the stuff just as she saw Adrian do the same. The merchant was pleased with their comments; he indicated towards several ornate, sealed bottles.

"If you like it, perhaps you would consider buying a few bottles to take along with you on your travels?"

Adrian grinned at the man as he handed him more money. "Or I might just buy a bottle to drink from tonight, and regret the migraine it gives me in the morning."

"I'm sure your lovely companion wouldn't want to deal with that," he replied, though he handed Adrian a bottle of wine nonetheless.

Scarlett could only laugh. "Trust me, I'll most likely have a headache alongside him. Have a good evening, sir."

The two of them visited a food stall next and bought smoked, salted potato dumplings and beef stew, before finding a vacant wooden table in the midst of a market square. The wood was gnarled and uneven, looking as if somebody had simply felled a tree, lain it on its side and declared their job of making a table complete. It made Scarlett think of Sam.

"I wonder how your woodcutter is doing," Adrian murmured. He finished his cup of wine in the space of a few seconds, then uncorked the bottle he'd bought and began swigging straight from it.

Scarlett stared at him. "I was just thinking of Sam, too. It's been a year since we've seen him."

"I'm sure he's working hard at ingratiating himself to your family, hoping your father realises that Sam is, in fact, the far superior match for his precious daughter than the wolf who stole her away."

"You don't mean that," she replied, swatting his arm in the process. The wine was already getting to Scarlett's head; along with the delicious food they were eating she was feeling altogether warm, hazy and satisfied.

Adrian raised an eyebrow. "Don't I?"

"Whether you genuinely do or not doesn't matter, anyway. It's hardly as if I'd rush back home crying that I'd made a terrible mistake in falling for a wolf."

"A wolf, you say?"

Adrian stilled at the voice. He turned just as Scarlett did the same. A dark-skinned woman who looked to be a few years older than Adrian was standing there, dressed resplendently in yellows and oranges and reds, like a flame. She had a cart with her full of bottles, scrolls and other miscellaneous items, some of which looked familiar to Scarlett.

"Are you a real witch, or a false one?" Adrian asked as he eyed the cart. Scarlett could tell by the twitch in his brow that he'd spied several items that he wished to have himself.

The woman smiled. "By the way you're looking at my potions I believe you already know. Though I'd prefer to be known a a witchdoctor, if it's all the same to you. I didn't spend years studying the art of healing to be reduced to a *witch.*" She regarded Adrian curiously. "So are you a wolf, sir, or aren't you?"

"I was, in a fashion, once upon a time. I'm not anymore."

The woman rummaged through her wares until she found a small, narrow vial filled with metallic-coloured liquid. "Once a wolf, always a wolf, I think. Would you like to see what I mean?"

Scarlett stared at her, trying hard to understand what the witchdoctor meant. "What does that potion do?" she asked, before talking a nervous gulp of wine.

"It reveals if a curse still lingers in one's blood," Adrian answered for her. He never took his eyes off the potion. The liquid danced in the light of the lanterns, sometimes gold, sometimes silver, but always beautiful. "Or a spell," he continued, "or any other kind of magic."

The witchdoctor was delighted by his answer. "You are a magician, sir."

"I am. What can I do to get my hands on some of that potion? I have been searching for a vial for a long time."

Scarlett straightened up in surprise. She hadn't known Adrian was looking for such a thing.

Does he want it for mere academic interest? she wondered. *I know he could identify its component ingredients if he had a sample to work with. Or does he want it for something else?*

The witchdoctor grinned at Adrian. She threw the vial at him and he caught it, quick as lightning. "You may have it, if you satisfy my curiosity by drinking some of it now."

"He can't do that!" Scarlett protested, getting to her feet, but Adrian pulled her back down.

"It's alright," he insisted. "The potion is only temporary. It merely serves to confirm whether there's anything hiding in one's blood, and nothing more."

"A phantom of a curse, as it were," the witchdoctor said, eyes gleaming. "If you truly were a wolf before, I would like to see if you're still capable of returning to the form tonight. Transformation magic is rare indeed; it would be a privilege to see it."

Scarlett did not like this one bit. The three of them had drawn a very curious audience, too; all around them were dozens of festival-goers, watching with fascinated eyes as Adrian unstoppered the vial and held it up to the light.

"Adrian," Scarlett began, "You are drunk. Surely this a terrible –"

"You underestimate how wonderful such a potion is, Red," he interrupted, a wolfish smile upon his face that Scarlett had not seen in months. "And you do not know how much I long to know if your grandmother's curse still lingers within me. And we have a crowd! We cannot disappoint such an eager audience, can we?"

The crowd cheered at Adrian's remark. Scarlett almost laughed at his showmanship – this was Adrian Wolfe, the merchant, at work. It was only then that she became aware that perhaps the witchdoctor had been hoping this would happen, for people were now rummaging through her cart with enthusiasm. If Adrian turned into a wolf using one of her potions then everyone would know her wares were genuine.

What a great marketing ruse, Scarlett thought, sighing as she drank more wine.

"Be careful, then," she said, resigned to Adrian's decision regardless of the consequences it might bring.

Adrian nodded, amber eyes flashing in the twilight. He downed half of the potion, then stoppered the vial before handing it over to Scarlett for safekeeping. He looked down at his waistcoat and began unbuttoning it.

"What are you –"

"I'm rather fond of this waistcoat," Adrian said, smirking. "And my boots, too. I'd rather they weren't destroyed...if I really do transform."

The next few minutes were fraught with tension, though a half-undressed Adrian kept gulping down wine as if there was nothing wrong whatsoever. The crowd grew restless, as did Scarlett.

Just as she concluded that nothing was going to happen, Adrian lurched forwards and fell to the cobbled floor, clutching at his chest with nails that were rapidly turning into claws. Scarlett wanted to look away; it was frightening to see the man she loved twist and morph into something else entirely, but she owed it to him to look. It was *her* grandmother who'd inflicted such a curse upon him, after all.

The crowd were rapt and afraid in equal measure.

As they should be, Scarlett thought. *They do not know if Adrian will be a friendly wolf, or a feral one.*

The witchdoctor, however, moved closer to Adrian. She bent down, taking note of every popping joint and broken bone and reformed limb as his body became less and less that of a man, and more and more that of a wolf.

Eventually, after several long minutes of shuddering and twitching, Adrian-the-wolf got to his feet. He was panting heavily, tongue lolling out of his mouth, casting his strange eyes across the crowd before fixing them on Scarlett.

They are not so strange when he is a wolf, she reasoned. *They fit him exactly as they should.*

When Adrian's tail began to wag and he gambolled over to Scarlett, the crowd burst into enthusiastic applause. The wolf was clearly no threat, though Adrian was large and strong, and his teeth long and terrible. But how could they feel threatened by a wolf who rubbed his head against Scarlett's hand, and nosed at her waist until she bent down to hug his neck?

"My, my," the witchdoctor said, "a tame wolf. You are certainly a strange one, magician."

"He was close to losing himself when we broke the curse before," Scarlett said, a small frown of worry creasing her brow. She glanced at the woman. "He won't do the same now, will he?"

She shook her head. "As I said before, this is a

phantom curse. Your love is in no danger...apart from the child about to grab his tail."

Scarlett laughed when she noticed the small boy reaching out for Adrian, who allowed him to touch him. He had always been great with children. He rolled onto his back, allowing the boy to scratch his stomach like a dog. The crowd couldn't seem to believe their eyes.

"He truly is a wolf," one man said.

"Look at the size of him!" said another.

A woman sighed. "But look how lovely he is!"

Even as a wolf they fall for him! Scarlett thought in disbelief. She traced a finger along Adrian's muzzle, ruffling his ears when he licked her hand and got back to his feet. When he stood up on his hind legs to reach the wine on the table Scarlett swiftly lifted the bottle away.

"None for you, Adrian," she teased, drinking from the bottle herself. "You had plenty before you transformed."

He whimpered, drawing several laughs from the crowd. Out of the corner of her eye Scarlett noticed the witchdoctor happily serving a hoard of customers; the woman would go to bed a very wealthy merchant.

"Shall we walk the streets, Adrian?" Scarlett suggested. The crowd murmured their agreement, and eagerly followed when Adrian padded forwards to lead the way.

The rest of the night was a blur of wine and lights and laughter. Scarlett had never seen Adrian enjoying himself as a wolf so much, though she supposed there had been nothing *fun* about his curse before. But now he was racing against confused yet happy street dogs, and play-fighting with big, burly men who relished the challenge of wrestling a wolf.

"This is certainly not a midsummer we're likely to forget," Scarlett told Adrian when they, finally, collapsed onto a bed in a nearby tavern, whose owner made an exception to allow Adrian to sleep there. It was hardly as if the man had ever had cause to give a wolf entry to his abode before, after all.

Adrian nibbled her ear as he curled up beside her. His large, fluffy tail covered Scarlett's legs, tickling her skin as he gently wagged it. She stroked his head.

"I could get used to this, you know," she said. "Wolf you is surprisingly good company. Though I still seemed to have to fend off interested young women."

Adrian merely stared at her. She giggled.

"I guess I *am* jealous. Good night, Adrian."

A lick across her face was his reply.

*

When Scarlett awoke Adrian was no longer a wolf, though he remained curled by her side where he had lain as one. He was watching her with eyes set alight by the

308

sunrise, a grin plastered to his face.

"What's got you in such a good mood?" she asked, rubbing at the promise of a headache within her temple. She really had drunk too much wine. "Now you know the wolf curse is still there, in your blood. We never really broke it."

To her surprise, Adrian laughed. "No, but now I also know there may be a way to control it. To flip it on and off, at will. The curse is there, dormant, merely waiting for me to do something with it."

"And what do you mean to do with it?"

"Who knows? I guess I'll have to find out."

"And how, exactly, will you do that?"

Adrian kissed her softly, his lips barely brushing against hers. She could feel him smiling.

"What do you think about searching for magic, Red?" he murmured. "Looking for cursed fools, and strange disappearances, and any number of wonderful things across the globe?"

Scarlett couldn't help but return Adrian's smile. He was never so handsome as he was when discussing magic.

"I'd say that sounds far more interesting that returning home, Mister Wolfe."

CHRONICLES OF CURSES BOOK TWO – SNOWSTORM KING

Kilian

It took Kilian precisely two minutes of consciousness to come to the conclusion that he didn't want to get out of bed. His head was killing him, he was freezing, and his shoulder ached from having slept on it badly. He glanced at the mostly-empty bottle of vodka lying on the floor and winced.

That was definitely full when I started drinking yesterday.

With a groan he threw himself back against his pillows. But just when Kilian decided that, as king, he could simply choose to remain in bed no matter what anybody said, he heard a knock on the door. He ignored it, of course, but it didn't go away.

"Who is it?!" he roared, immediately regretting having shouted when his head rang painfully in response.

"Your Royal Highness, the messenger from Alder is seeking an audience again," came the timid voice of a servant Kilian didn't care to recognise the voice of.

"Send her away," he replied, waving a dismissive hand at the door even though the servant couldn't see it.

"Ah, you see, Your Royal Highness," the man said hesitantly, "as regent you really are obligated to listen to the spokespeople of your country, and this is the fifth time you've turned her away –"

"I am aware of my obligations," Kilian bit back. He rubbed his head. "Fine then. Don't turn her away, but don't let her in, either. Let me see what she will do whilst blatantly being ignored."

He could tell the servant didn't like Kilian's response one bit, but he didn't care. Shivering as he forced himself out of bed, he threw on a long overcoat that lay abandoned on the floor, staring dolefully at the blackened, empty fireplace opposite his bed in the process. He was about to call out for his personal servant to see to getting a new fire started, but then Kilian remembered that he'd fired him.

He'd fired most of the castle staff, truth be told. He couldn't stand them. All hired by his father or his older brother. All of them judging every disappointing move Kilian made as if they expected nothing more from him than self-indulgent depravity.

Well, if that's what they expected then that's what

they'd get. Kilian had kept on barely enough staff to keep torches lit and food cooking in the kitchen. He enjoyed the solitude. If he could get away with it he'd have fired every last soul in the castle – including himself.

Kilian never wanted to be king, even in a temporary capacity, and he wanted it even less now it had been forced upon him.

Staggering over to the tall window in his room, which overlooked the grounds to the front of the castle and allowed him to gaze across the forest to the town of Alder, Kilian felt his mood worsen. The weather was truly awful – the last time it had been this bad he'd been just three years old. That time, the winter had been despicable simply through bad luck. The current bout of bad weather had nothing to do with luck, bad or otherwise, just like the twenty years of *good* winters that preceded it.

Kilian didn't want to think about that.

Clutching his overcoat tighter around himself against the cold, he gazed down to the heavy iron front doors of the castle. A woman stood there, huddled into her cloak and looking thoroughly miserable. This was, indeed, the fifth time in as many days that the messenger from Alder had coming seeking an audience with Kilian. He had to admire her tenacity.

I suppose the town must be getting desperate, he thought, looking up at the endless white sky and its blinding, heavy snow. *The weather has been awful ever since my father died, and it's my fault. Not that I care. If they die that's one less thing for me to pretend to worry about.*

All Kilian had to do was keep the throne warm for his brother's return. Gabriel had been at war since summer, fighting in the borders for some reason or other that Kilian had never deemed important enough to remember. Any day now he'd come back – triumphant or otherwise – and Kilian would be free of his responsibilities. He could leave the castle. Leave the country. He could go wherever he wanted.

In the meantime he was stuck inside a miserable, never-ending snowstorm. How could anyone expect him to *actually* do his job well when he'd never wanted it? His father should never have forced the position onto his youngest son if he'd wanted the kingdom taken care of.

But his father was dead and his brother gone. Now all Kilian could do was try to wrangle out some form of amusement to fill his days until he was free of the damn castle.

And I guess she'll have to do, he thought, a sly smile on his face as he gazed once more down at the woman in her blue cloak, almost invisible through the blizzard.

Kilian threw off his overcoat just long enough to dress in a white shirt and pair of leggings before sliding the coat back on top; his teeth were already chattering by the time he huddled against the fabric once more. His head was still killing him, so Kilian picked up the mostly-empty bottle of vodka from the floor and swallowed what was left. Fighting the immediate urge to vomit, he laced on a pair of boots, dragged a hand through his long, unkempt hair and slammed his door open.

Nobody was in the corridor, as expected. He wondered if he'd have to stop by the kitchen in order to get something for the pain in his head, though Kilian did not possess the patience to do so. When he reached the throne room he collapsed onto the overly-decorated chair, swinging his legs over one of the armrests as he dipped his head back over the other.

"Bring her in!" he called out to nobody in particular; he wasn't sure if anybody was even within earshot. "And get me some wine. In fact, bring me wine before you bring the girl." Kilian had priorities, after all, even if nobody else agreed with them. His first and foremost priority was always to be as drunk as he could physically get away with being, and he was at least a bottle of wine too sober for his own tastes.

A scrabbling by the door to the throne room told Kilian that his orders had been heard. Impatiently he waited for someone to bring his alcohol. When they did it was accompanied by bread, meats and cheeses. He waved that away.

"Did I say I needed food?" he demanded. But, upon feeling his stomach pinch in response, he waved the servant back. "Never mind. Keep it here. Now go away and fetch the girl."

Kilian scratched his chin as he guzzled down his first goblet of wine. A fine layer of stubble was growing; he needed to shave. He hadn't had cause to do so for days, though.

When was the last time I had a woman? he wondered. It had been at least two weeks. Resolving to have one sent to his rooms later that day, he shifted slightly on the throne when the sound of soft, light footsteps made their way towards him.

When the woman pulled down her snow-covered hood Kilian froze.

"Your R-Royal Highness," she said, shivering heavily as she struggled to bow. "M-my name is Elina Brodeur, and I c-come on behalf of Alder to seek your help."

But he wasn't listening. Kilian had never seen a woman like Elina Brodeur from his own country before. She stood out, dark and strange against the snow, reminding him of a man who had once come to the castle twenty years ago.

He straightened up on the throne and cleared his throat.

"You're the magician's girl."

*

316

ACKNOWLEDGEMENTS

Oh, wow. I finally finished another book!

For those who are picking up **Big, Bad Mister Wolfe** as their first book by me, hello! I'm so happy you decided to read my story. My first novel was written back in 2015, and it was published two years later. I think my writing has improved dramatically since then...I hope (though I still love my first book; it's my baby!).

I've always wanted to write a fairy tale. Or, at the very least, retell a fairy tale. I hope I did **Red Riding Hood** justice. And I hope you love **Adrian Wolfe**! I thought long and hard about how exactly I wanted to portray him. He's a smarmy git, but I love him.

As with any of my writing endeavours I could not have completed this novel without the unwavering critical and emotional support of my editor, Kirsty Campbell, and my partner, Jake. They are the backbone upon which I stay up all night writing and fall into bed at seven in the morning, exhausted.

Many thanks of course to my family and friends, who share my books everywhere and love me very much. I could not have made it this far through a dramatic career change without each and every one of them.

And finally, of course, I would like to thank anyone who decided to pick up this book and read it. I sincerely hope you enjoyed it as much as I loved writing it.

Here's to many more,

Hayley

ABOUT THE AUTHOR

Hayley Louise Macfarlane hails from the very tiny hamlet of Balmaha on the shores of Loch Lomond in Scotland. Having spent eight years studying at the University of Glasgow and graduating with a BSc (hons) in Genetics and then a PhD in Synthetic Biology, Hayley quickly realised that her long-term passion for writing trumped her desire to work in a laboratory.

Now Hayley spends her time writing across a whole host of genres. After spending much of 2019 writing fairy tales she'll be branching into apocalyptic science fiction, paranormal & urban fantasy and maybe even a touch of horror in 2020. But never fear: the fairy tales won't be away for long!

During 2019, Hayley set herself the ambitious goal of publishing one thing every month. Seven books, two novellas, two short stories and one box set later, she made it. She recommends that anyone who values their sanity and a sensible sleep cycle does not try this.

Printed in Great Britain
by Amazon